Always in My Heart

CARRIE J. KEATON

ISBN
978-1-956529-68-5 (Paperback)
978-1-956529-67-8 (eBook)

Carrie J. Keaton

14663 Highway 86 Holly Grove, AR 72069

(H) 870-659-5330 or (Message Phone) 870-830-0218

Table of Contents

Chapter 1

"**R**achel Pendleton, you are really pathetic. You are sitting here in this huge, plush office with a career a lot of people would die for, but you have no special someone with whom you can share all of your triumphs and good fortune, she thought to herself as she stared out of her office window.

She had recently moved back to her hometown of Manhattan from Philadelphia where she had lived for the past ten years. She had worked at the Philadelphia Chronicle, which is a wonderful, averaged-sized, Philadelphia magazine company.

Rachel's mind revisited her time spent at the Philadelphia magazine company. She had been a very detail-oriented editor at the company and most of her days started out early, but she had so enjoyed writing and meeting the deadlines. Often she would put in long workdays because she took such great pride in her work. It was nothing for her to put in a seventy-hour workweek because she was single and had no children and had an almost nonexistent personal life.

As time went on, she had lost count of the many times her friends, colleagues, and family members had tried to play cupid for her. Her mother topped the list though of all the matchmakers. Mrs. Pendleton is a 58 year old who is young at heart, a proud mother of two grown daughters (Rachel 27 and Robin 31). She is a true Scorpio... devoted, loyal, playful and loving... all with the fire of passion. She likes to have targets in life and then to reach them, prefer telling people the truth, loves helping everybody she can, and has a great sense of humor. Mr. Pendleton is quiet, reserved man who loves his family and just supports whatever or whoever that makes his daughters happy. Rachel's mom is a bit pushy in trying to get the last of her two daughters married because she believes that family should be placed above a career. Rachel's dear mom was relentless in trying to hook her daughter up with someone who she thought would be a good match for her. She was always preaching to her about how she was just wasting her life away, that she going to be an old maid and that there is more to life than work. Rachel did try dating some of these guys that her mom selected for her, but to date, she had not clicked with anyone. Rachel's personal opinion of the whole thing was that she felt like she was a desirable enough woman to find my own man if she really and truly wanted one. Most of the time, Rachel would just go back to her usual mode — that she's too busy to have a man in her life right now. Having a relationship is just simply too much work was what she would tell herself.

Finally Rachel had gotten a well-earned promotion for her exceptional writing talent. She had gotten promoted to a bigger office in one of the parent companies of the Philadelphia Chronicle, the Manhattan Times Review in Manhattan, New York. She had hoped that moving back to Manhattan and being so much more closer to her mom would not be a huge mistake, but her promotion was an once-in-a-lifetime chance she could not pass up so easily. She would be the managing editor at the company and have her own expense account and car. The promotion was a great career opportunity for her, a chance to be home again and return to her old stumping ground, be near some of her old friends and family.

Rachel's assistant knocking on her door broke her reverie and brought her back to the present.

"Hey — you have a call from someone named Roman Sinclair. Do you want to take it?"

"Yeah — sure — I'll take it. Thanks Tina."

"Are you sure Rachel? You look a little surprised. I can tell him that you are in a meeting or something if you want."

"No, that's okay Tina. It will be alright; I just had not spoken to him in a long time -- but thank you," Rachel said trying to smile a little more confidently.

Roman Sinclair had been a close friend to her since fourth grade, but the two of them had somewhat drifted apart since their college days. Her friends and his had always called him *Romey.*

"Well hello Roman — what's going on?"

"What's happening lady — how are you doing?'

"I'm good — I'm good, but how did you find me?"

"I'm a resourceful man. Oh -- by the way, congratulations on your promotion. I always knew that you would do great things Rachel. And to answer your question about how I found you – You should know that anything that I want found will be found or have you forgotten that?"

"Yes, I guess I did forget you are like a bloodhound."

"Hoooooowwwwl," Romey said playfully.

"It's been so long since we talked Romey that I don't know what to say. Are you okay?" Rachel asked, creasing her brow with concern.

"I was hoping that maybe you would agree to have dinner with me this Saturday night so that we can catch up on things. I really need to talk to you Rachel."

"Sure Romey, we can have dinner and catch up. That might be nice," I Rachel said, a smile slowly adorning her face.

"Alright then -- So what time should we meet?"

"How about seven o'clock and we can meet at the Yuca Bar across from Tompkins Square Park."

"I remember that place – great Mexican food. I'll see you then Rachel."

After hanging up the phone, Rachel's mind entered a portal in time when she and Romey were growing up in Manhattan. Both of us loved the music of the 70's and 80's because we grew up with it. This type of music was real music to us. Some of the rap music was okay, but our hearts was with the 70's and 80's Motown and R & B. We got our groove on to the Chi-lites, Tyrone Davis, Johnny Taylor, The Temptations, Marvin Gaye, The Isley Brothers, The O'Jays, Aretha Franklin, Main Ingredient, Atlantic Star, Angela Bofill, Gladys Knight and the Pips, New Birth, The Persuaders, the Spinners, and many more artists.

Rachel remembered a time in she and Romey's teen years; they around fourteen, when Romey's voice had gone through the change. He used to sing to her on all of her birthdays. His voice had been higher pitched when he sung to her. After Romey's voice changed, it acquired a richer, expressive, baritone nature. Just the sound of his voice when he sung to her moved her in ways that she didn't understand. She told him then that she believed that he could become a famous singer like some of our favorite male vocalists like: Marvin Gaye, Luther Vandross, Peabo Bryson, Teddy Pendergrass, James Ingram, Barry White, Jeffrey Osborne, Eddie Levert, Bobby Womack, and Freddie Jackson just to name a few. Romey would only shy away from any comment that she made comparing his vocal talent to these great artists. But Rachel was really serious about his singing. He had talent but he just didn't realize it. Since he was her friend, she would never let him forget about his singing ability. It's was funny how they had told each other everything and had never been romantically involved, but they had kept their relationship strictly plutonic. Rachel did recall a time when they were in college when the two of them had gotten caught up and shared a kiss. Things never went any further and they never spoke about it again.

Soft knocking on my door interrupted my thoughts.

"Rachel – I'm leaving now unless you need something," Tina said.

"No Tina, I don't need anything – you go on and leave okay? Have a great weekend," she replied.

About a half hour after Tina and the others had gone home, Rachel decided she should call it quits for the day and leave too. Maybe the girls night out would be fun and keep my mind off of Romey.

After work and on almost each Friday, Rachel and her girlfriends met at Charley's in downtown Manhattan around seven thirty or eight to celebrate the arrival of the weekend. When Rachel arrived and pulled up in front of the restaurant, she smiled happily and checked her makeup and touched up her lipstick before stepping out of her red corvette.

After getting out of her car, she set the alarm. The car made its usual loud beep-beep sound that startled a couple walking pass her. The guy turned and looked back at Rachel as they passed, admiring her five-foot seven-inch, caramel colored frame walk into the restaurant.

"What are you looking at?" the woman screamed at him.

He tried to make excuses for his behavior, but the woman continued yelling at him. Rachel had heard the commotion, but just continued walking.

Rachel stepped inside of Charley's, which always had dimly lit lights and the music playing was soft and mellow. Everyone was talking, laughing, and eating. The usual guys were at the bar trying to pick up women. As I watched the people here, I was a bit envious of them because of the heavy workload I had; hell, I wouldn't have the time to date if I wanted to.

As she slowly walked through the restaurant, she saw a hand waving at her from across the room. It was Courtney, and right next to her was Pam.

"Hey girl — you took your time getting here!" Courtney playfully mocked, as Rachel approached the table. "Are you sure you're not hiding a man out somewhere?" Pam said with a mischievous glint in her eyes.

"With all the problems you have with guys Pam, I need to remain single," Rachel shot back with mock attitude. "Have you guys been waiting long?"

"Not very long Rachel — maybe about ten minutes or so," Courtney replied, as she seated herself.

"Good evening — would you like to order your drink now?" a waiter said, breaking up our light-hearted raillery.

"Yes I do," Rachel replied. "I'll have a cognac with sparkling water and lemon."

"Will do," the waiter said, as he left to fill my order.

"Hey, he's kind of fine," Pam admired.

"Yeah — but he's not Rachel's type," Courtney added.

"Rachel is strong and independent. She needs someone who makes some decent money and isn't intimidated by a successful woman Pam."

"The fact that this guy is a waiter shouldn't matter if he treats Rachel right," Pam snapped back.

"Okay ladies — let's chill out. I appreciate what you are trying to do here, but I just don't have time for a man," Rachel said with a contented smile. "Let's just have fun and enjoy our night — and talk about something other than my love life or my lack of one."

"You know Rachel — you're not getting any younger and —

"Hey — stop it. I'm happy just as I am. After all, it's my life to live as I choose. Now let's leave this matchmaking thing alone, okay?" Rachel remarked a bit harshly.

Courtney sensed the tone in my voice and quickly changed the subject.

"Are you ladies ready to order from the menu now?" the waiter spoke with a pleasant smile, while placing my drink on the table.

"I would," Rachel replied. "I'd like a grilled chicken salad with a serving of garlic bread."

"I'll have a rib eye steak, baked potato, and an ear of corn," Courtney said right after I had ordered.

"I want an order of ribs, potato logs, and baked beans," Pam said, eyeing the expression displayed on my face.

"Rachel — why did you ignore the waiter like that? You wouldn't even look him in the face and he was clearly being friendly with you. He was checking you out and you just paid him no mind," Pam said after the waiter had walked away.

"Rachel — I know you don't want to hear no more talk about us trying to fix you up, but we just care about you girl. Hey — you got needs too. What's wrong with getting you some sometimes?" Pam remarked, with a mischievous smile.

"I'll get my needs met — just not at this point in my life. I just don't have time — I'm too busy," I said defensively.

"Well, it wouldn't hurt you to get out and enjoy yourself every once in a while. A man's company wouldn't hurt," Courtney said, as we ate.

"Hey — I know — you can take a trip somewhere," Pam added.

"Taking a trip really wouldn't apply to me. A lot of people take trips to get away from their co-workers and their jobs. I just happen to love both my job and my co-workers. Besides, I get to travel around everywhere on assignment," I said smiling at them and knowing that I'd made a good case.

After our meal, we paid and left Charley's.

"Someone please tell me how come we all work at the same magazine, but no one has a fly ride but Rachel," Pam said in mock jealousy, as they stood and marveled my shiny red sports car.

"Everybody can't be a top-notch editor and we all have husbands and children," Courtney replied teasingly.

"Both of you have great men by your sides, beautiful children, and great lives. You all know that you wouldn't trade all of that for anything, now would you?" Rachel replied, raising her brow and smirking at the two of them.

I gave both my friends a big hug.

"I'll see you at work Monday morning Courtney and you behave yourself girl, Rachel replied.

"And Rachel, try to get you some soon, okay?" Pam said, waving good-bye as she headed for the subway entrance.

Courtney said her final good-byes and ran to catch up to Pam.

Rachel glanced at her watch. It was very late and she wasn't really ready to go home, but she had no place else to go. After giving the idea some thought, she decided to go home anyway.

On the drive home, Rachel admired Manhattan's bustle. She was making a great career right here for herself and had great friends. She enjoyed the stimulation and the energy that Manhattan possessed and it was the place to be in her opinion.

As Rachel approached Lansing Boulevard, she exited the freeway and headed for the underground garage, then took the elevator to her fifth floor apartment. After unlocking the door and turning on the lights, she made her way to her spacious bedroom and plopped down on her bed. Kicking her shoes off, she lay back on her bed and said to herself, *girl --you are so pathetic to not have someone special in your life.* She had chosen to have a career over trying to have a personal life. Rachel's mind drifted back to what Courtney and Pam had said at dinner about having a man in her life. She wondered if they were right. *Did she really need a man in her life she thought?* She had a wonderful career that she was successful at and that she loved so what else could she possibly need? But realistically, she knew deep down that she would like to marry someday, just not right now. Her friends seem to make such a big deal out of having someone special in her life, but with her, that idea always seemed to come in second place.

Rachel decided to dismiss the thought of having a relationship from her mind, and opted to run herself a hot, bubble bath in the sunken tub. After starting the water, she adjusted it to her favorite temperature, and added jasmine scented salts and foam bath gelee. She went to the dresser and got her favorite black, silk teddy with matching robe to put on after her long, hot bath. On the way back, she paused at her bed, closed her eyes and entertained the thought of having someone to share her bed with. *Yes — it would be wonderful to share my bed with someone special*, she admitted to herself, while opening her eyes and shaking her head in despair.

Rachel eased into the tub and allowed the warm, scented water relax her tired body. All of the muscles in her body felt tense, but she didn't know why. Her mind kept thinking back on all the people who had tried to be matchmaker and fix her up with their brothers, moms, colleagues, and their friends. Even her own mom had been trying to put her with some of her friend's sons or someone at her church. *Why was everyone trying so hard to fix my life? Maybe it was me. Maybe there is something wrong with me and my way of thinking and everyone can see it except me. No — no — no — they can't be right. This is my life she said to herself. I will live it the way I please. I know what's best for me.*

Pam and Courtney's words at dinner continued to haunt Rachel, regardless of how she tried to brush them from her thoughts. She sank deeper into the tub, trying to erase any notion of her wanting or needing a man right now. She told herself that having a family life would only hold her back.

Rachel stayed in the tub a little while longer, and then decided to get out. After she had gotten dressed, the phone suddenly rang.

"Hi there Rachel, how are you?" the familiar voice echoed through the phone.

"I'm good Michael, and how are you?

"Oh I'm just wonderful. I was just giving you a call to make sure you hadn't gotten my message about me going out of town for a few days. You will be okay with running the office while I'm gone won't you?"

Michael Flannigan is my boss at the Manhattan Times Review.

"Yes — of course — I will be fine – everything will be fine," I said in a reassuring voice.

"Okay Rachel— you have a good night then okay, and I'll see you in a few days, probably late Wednesday afternoon okay? Bye."

After hanging up with Michael, Rachel still wasn't sleepy. She thought that the hot bath would have done the trick but it didn't. She had been back in Manhattan for nearly two weeks but still had some unpacking left undone.

So she decided to finish the rest of the unpacking tonight. Once she had finished the rest of her unpacking, she was beat and decided to shower and go to bed. Tomorrow would be a new day.

Chapter 2

It was Saturday and Rachel was anticipating seeing Romey, wondering how he looked and wondering what he wanted to talk to her about. It didn't really matter to her what their conversation was about as long as she got the chance to stare into his handsome face. It's downright shameful to be crushing on someone the way she on Roman Sinclair.

Loud knocking interrupted her sensuous thoughts. "Hey… open up girl and let your cousin in. It's been a minute since I've seen you Rach," Valerie yelled through the door.

Rachel hesitantly went to the door and opened it and there stood her cousin Val eyeing her up and own mischievously over the top of her shades.

Valerie strolled briskly by Rachel and spun around on her heel. Throwing both arms around her Val quickly squeezes and lifts Rachel off the floor in a bear hug. Val places her back on the floor. "I'm so happy to see you Rach."

Rachel quickly gets her bearing and responds, "It's great seeing you too Valerie. Uh-h –h it has been a few years hasn't it?"

"Yeah Rach it has been a while. I wanted to ask you if you got plans for tonight?"

"I suppose to meet up with Romey to talk."

"Rach why did you never own your feeling for your boy Romey? You know you been feeling him for a long time."

"I just never had the nerve to do that Val… I was always too afraid of what he might think of me."

"So you would just rather see some other woman be with him than to stake your own claim and tell him how you really feel."

"Val you know I just can't……"

"Yeah… I'm gonna leave alone Rach. I know. You scared. He might not feel the way you feel. I done heard it all before. Enjoy your day with Romey. I'll holla at you later."

After Valerie left Rachel pondered over she and Val's conversation about Romey. She knew Val was right and that she should be honest about her feelings. But for now Rachel feels it isn't the time to make known her true feeling to Romey.

Around four-thirty that evening, Rachel showered, dressed and left for her dinner date with Romey. She was the type of person who mostly arrived at a destination early so she had made it to the Yuca Bar first. She seated herself at the bar and ordered a white strawberry sangria because she loved the strawberries that was mixed into this drink.

The Yuca Bar was a great Mexican restaurant offering a delectable mix of South of the Border delights in a pleasant atmosphere. Yuca is a popular, reasonably priced date place. Groups are welcome too, but reservations may be needed during the evening. The bar offers a happy hour every day. You could take a seat by the window and watch the world go by or sit in an isolated area to dine. Specialty cocktails, wines, and Sangria provide some nice choices to compliment the meal.

Romey was fifteen minutes late and Rachel was a little annoyed at him for making her wait. But her annoyance was soon replaced by awe after she finally laid eyes on him. He was a one fine hunk of a man with a killer smile.

Spinning around on the bar stool, Rachel was now face to face with her handsome friend which she had not seen in nearly ten years. She slid off the stool and positioned herself so that she could take in the full affect of his presence.

"Rachel – you look great. I'm so happy to see you," Romey said, throwing his arms around her tightly.

"Rachel's arms encircled his muscular waist as she took in his overwhelmingly masculine smell. *Damn this man smells so good and feels so good she thought to herself. Get a grip girl -- get yourself together she scolded."*

"You look great too Romey, but you are late," Rachel said, pulling away from his grip and pretending to be angry.

"I know Rach – I'm sorry. Can we get a table?"

"Oh I guess so. Come on you big lug," she said, taking him by the hand and pulling him toward a vacant table over in an isolated corner of the restaurant. Romey and I ordered sangria and vegetable tapas that were absolutely delicious. We had a wonderfully fun time, and to see us together, you would think we had been together all these years. It's funny how that goes, sometimes. You don't see a person for many years, but the connections you made way back when seem to remain intact. We reminisced and named names, laughed and compared notes and shared updates on our lives thus far. It was good to catch up and I secretly hoped that we'd stay in touch this time.

After dinner, Romey and I took a stroll arm in arm down West 71st Street toward the Jazz Depot.

"Hey Rachel – I got a surprise for you. Do you know where we are headed?

I had not really noticed the direction in which the two of us were headed because I was just enjoying the night air and the ambience of the evening. I had not been back in Manhattan for quite some time so I had to get my bearings on our location.

A warm flush washed over me as the memories of a familiar place from the past came rushing back.

"The Jazz Depot – The Jazz Depot. OMG! It's been so long since I had been there – since my high school and college years. So it is still here?" I asked excitedly.

"Well yes it is," Romey stated.

As we rounded the next corner, there it stood in all of its glory.

"It's just as I remember."

"Only better," Romey added.

"You know, I remember when you used to sing a little and danced in the theatre and you were quite good."

"Romey you were the one with the voice that would go places. I always told you that and I still believe that too."

My mind revisited the days in my past that I danced and sang. It was a wonderful time in my life. Now that we are all living in the world of emails, Facebook, YouTube, MySpace, Reunion, etc., sooner or later old friends will locate you. Sometimes it can be a pleasant situation, and at other times, being discovered by an old "friend" can be a pain. This past week, however, I had been hearing from several of my friends from my Broadway days in New York City; in this case, my "Chorus Line" buddies. It had been a joy to hear from them. The conversations proved to be quite interesting, as we took a stroll down memory lane. We reminisced about the look and feel of New York City in the 1970's, which is totally different now, especially since 911. We spoke about our non-stop rehearsals from morning till night, locking the choreography in our minds and in our bodies.

For the record, the original production of A Chorus Line opened in 1975 at the Shubert Theatre, located in the famous Shubert Alley. The late Michael Bennett, who conceived, directed and choreographed the show, also had a big hand in the shaping of the music composed by Academy Award and Grammy-winner, Marvin Hamlish, who collaborated with lyricist Ed Kleban. The book was authored by Nicolas Dante and James Kirkwood, Jr. Hamlisch is remembered for his 1974 Academy Awards for the mainstream success of Barbara Streisand's The Way We Were and of course, the Broadway score of A Chorus Line, for which he won the Tony Award and the Pulitzer Prize Award.

Michael Bennett was a brilliant man, who, at the time, was being pursued by Hollywood film moguls, television brass, record executives and publishing houses; he was the King of Broadway. While still in the cast of the Broadway show, performing nightly, Mr. Bennett told me that he was going to record me on MCA Records, as part of a new deal he signed with them. He was the first to record me as a solo artist. We released a record titled Swept Away in Love on MCA Records, written by Bobby Thomas, the drummer for the show. When I look back on the phenomenon that A Chorus Line was, it brings back so many mind-boggling moments of my friends on Broadway and the wonderful experiences we shared.

We enjoyed being the toast of Broadway, and we all learned so much sitting by Michael's side watching him put this classic musical on its feet. Though we have lost some of the cast members over the years, I am pleased to note that many are still with us and now their kids are involved in the theatre – a chip off the old block, I'd say.

The evening with my old friend Roman Sinclair was great and filled with hope and promise. Who knows what the future holds and just maybe I'd get to see more of him since I'd moved back to Manhattan. Who knows – maybe we will finally have a chance to see where our relationship could go.

Chapter 3

Manhattan did have its appeal. Rachel had not lived here in over ten years, but during her brief period here back then she had worked in a public relations firm. Now she was living here again and had set up her new place of residence. As she stood by the fireplace mantel admiring a photo of her mom and her sister Robin, she remembered how she and her mom had spent a whole day unpacking and placing things in her apartment. Her mom was such an incurable matchmaker and had been constantly trying to fix her up with some of her friends' sons. She checked in with Rachel nearly every day and was over at Rachel's apartment for a visit today.

"Rachel I'm so glad that you're back. You know what? I'm gonna set you up on a date with Marion's nephew Orlando. He is really a very handsome young man and —

"Stop it Mama — please," Rachel said, holding up her hand.

All right — Rachel — All right! Well then, answer this question for me. Have you talked to Romey lately?" Mama asked, giving me a curious eye and observing my face for an expression.

"Yes — why do you ask?"

"Hey, I was just curious. You know Rachel — I still think you and Romey would be good together. Tell me honey girl — have you and Romey ever — well — you know – get together?" Mama asked, raising a brow in curiosity.

"Whoa-a-a-a Mama. Romey and I are just friends — we're just friends Mama. The two of us have been friends since we were eight years old. There has never been anything romantic between us Mama."

"You and Romey never even came close to doing it? Come on Rachel! I have already been where you are going. You and he never even got a little smoochie smooch in here and there?" Mama asked, playfully smushing her lips together.

"Well — maybe just a little kiss — once," Rachel confessed.

"I knew it! I knew it! When was Rachel? When did Romey and you kiss?" Mama inquired.

"Oh Mama — it was years ago — back when we was in college. It never went any further. We just dismissed it like it never happened. We never brought it up again."

Mama stood there with her arms folded, patting her foot and observing my facial expressions as I talked. I continued talking, stammering in my speech, trying to cover the fact that I have feelings for Romey. I could tell though that Mama wasn't buying my story.

"So you are telling me that you never thought about getting together with Romey at all?"

"Yeah — well — he asked me once — you know — about us getting together, but I told him that I didn't think it was such a good idea."

"What! — Rachel! — I know you didn't just turn him down like that!"

"Well Mama — I thought that it would ruin our friendship if it didn't work out."

"Honey girl, I just can't believe that you did that," Mama said, shaking her head in disbelief.

"Well — you know Mama — relationships come and go. But real friendships lasts a lifetime."

"Whatever you say sweetie – I'll leave it alone for now. Okay?"

"You know Romey and me are better off just being friends. I've known him seem like forever and we talk about everything. I just don't want to take a chance on losing that Mama."

"Okay Rachel — all right? I'll leave it as you say for now. But I still think that you got a thing for Romey I don't care what you say."

I gave Mom the evil eye, but with a playful smile. I knew that mama meant well — especially with Romey and me.

"Hey — Rachel — look, I got to go and run some errands. I'll see you at home tonight for dinner, okay?" Mama said, as she was leaving.

After Mama had gone, my mind wandered to a time when Romey and me were kids growing up in the Bronx. Things were so different back then. People probably don't think about it much now, but throughout the 70's and 80's, Motown really was the sound of a lot of teenage America. Many of America's memory from the 70's time period had been comprised of a list of Motown hits. Though many of us didn't realize it, song hits like *"Ain't No Mountain High Enough, Bernadette, Stop in the Name of Love, I Was Made to Love Her, My Guy, and My Girl*, all came from the same hit factory. Of course Motown wasn't the only center of the vigorous African-American music scene in the 70's. Influential A-sides were cut by Stax-Volt artists like Aretha Franklin, Otis Redding, Sam and Dave, and Booker T and the MG's; by semi-independent acts like the Isley Brothers, and Sly and the Family Stone; and of course, by the one man the music industry came to know as James Brown. This Motown magic had taken Romey and I on a musical journey through the 1970's and 80's Motown and soul music.

She was jolted back to reality when a glass that I was holding slipped from my hand and crashed on the hardwood floor. I looked down at the glass, which was scattered across the floor in a million pieces. Getting the broom and dustpan, I cleaned up the mess and finished putting the rest of my glasses in the cabinet.

By now, it had turned into late evening. It wasn't long before the party will start and I needed to get ready. I selected a form-fitting, burgundy dress from my closet that accentuated my ample figure.

"Who knows — I mumbled to myself. I may meet some eligible guys at this party. I guess it doesn't hurt to be prepared just in case."

After showering, I dressed and did my hair up in an upsweep, leaving a few select, curly tendrils hanging loosely about. As I was putting the finishing touches to my make-up, the doorbell rang.

When I opened the door, Val was standing there with a playful smirk on her face.

"Nice dress Rachel — you clean up nicely."

"You look nice too Val," I replied. "Come on in."

"You're dressing up for Romey aren't you? You know that he's going to be there."

"Girl no — I'm not. I told you Val — we're just friends," I replied innocently.

"Whatever — come on girl. Let's go and get our party on."

When Val and I arrived at the party, it was already in full swing. People were everywhere — dancing, laughing, talking, and eating. As Val and I walked pass a couple of guys, they were gawking at us.

"Hello sweet thang. I bet you can rock my world," one of the guys managed to slur out.

"Yeah right — in your dreams," Val snapped back.

Val and I looked at each other and burst out laughing.

"You know they are just losers Rachel."

"I know — see, that's what I'm talking about Val. This is why I stay single. Guys can't seem to get their shit together. Hell, I don't have time for that kind of drama."

"Forget those guys Rach. Don't sweat it. Let's grab us a couple of drinks and get our groove on girl."

As soon as we had gotten our drinks, a guy approached us and asked Val to dance. He reached out and took her hand and was urging her to come and dance with him.

"Hey girl, I'm going to start getting my groove on now," she said, prancing about on her way to dance.

I seated myself at the bar and just sat there smiling at Val and sipping on my drink. Looking around, I could see that mostly everyone was having a great time. Somehow, through the large crowd of people and directly in front of me, my eyes fell upon Romey. As always, he was the center of attention and just as handsome as ever. I smiled contently to myself, and admired every inch of his fine frame. With a killer smile, sexy eyes, and his smooth ebony skin, it was easy to see why women flocked to him. Romey was also very intelligent and a shrewd businessman.

Finally, he looks in my direction and notices me watching him. I waved at Romey and burst into a huge smile. He made his way through the crowd to greet me.

"What's up Rach? Woman, you look so damned good! Just look at you! Give me a hug!" he cried out, grabbing me and pulling me into his arms.

"Hello Romey. It's been a while hasn't it?" I bubbled with adoration.

"Show you right — it's been too long," he said, hugging me again.

While we were hugging, a woman approaches us smiling.

"Romey, is this Rachel?" she asks in a slightly raised tone.

"Yes — yes — this is Rachel Pendleton — a dear, dear friend," Romey said, with much enthusiasm. "Rachel— this is Franchesca Devine, my fiancée."

"It is so nice to meet you — and please — call me Frannie. Romey talks about you all the time."

"I hope that all the things that Romey has been telling you weren't bad things," I said, as we shook hands.

"Oh no Rachel — of course not. Everything that I've heard about you has been wonderful. I really admire your work."

"Thank you — Frannie," I said modestly. "I love those earrings."

"Thanks girl. Romey bought these for my birthday," Frannie said, as she snuggling up closer to Romey.

"Your dress is beautiful. That color really compliments you Rachel."

"Come on Frannie — let's go dance," Romey said, pulling her by the hand.

"See you later Rach," he said, with a playful wink.

"Talk to you later," Frannie yelled back to me, as she was being pulled away.

I walked back over to the bar and seated myself and asked the bartender to freshen my drink. As I sipped my drink, I admired Romey as he and Frannie slow danced. He'd turned into quite a man over the years. Deep down, I knew that I loved him — truth is that I have always loved him, for years. But he is my best friend — my homey. We've shared everything together since childhood and have always been there for each other as friends.

After finishing my drink, I decided that I would go home. Just about everyone was paired off with someone except me. It was time for me to go. I waved at Val and headed home.

When I arrived home, I was still reminiscing about Romey and me. It wasn't right for me to be thinking or feeling this way about him. After all, he and I are only friends. I had to try to shake these thoughts and feelings somehow.

Then I thought — I still had some unpacking left that needs to be done. So I pulled out several boxes and began placing their contents where they needed to go. After a short time, my mind trailed back off once again to Romey and Frannie. I thought — she was kind of close to the type of women Romey's usually attracted to. He always seemed to be drawn to the hoochie-mama types with the tight, short dresses and the long fake nails — you know — the kind of women that you would see in some of those music videos today. Frannie seemed to want to be a high-class chick.

The ringing doorbell snapped me back to the present. When I answered the door, it was Val.

"Girl, why did you leave," she asked in a slightly agitated tone. "I knew you came back here and would be probably feeling sorry for yourself."

Val followed me into my apartment, closing the door behind her.

"Well everyone was having such a great time and I didn't have anyone to be with, so I came home."

"You ought to have been with Romey instead of that old floozy that was hanging all over him," Val ranted.

"That old floozy as you call her happens to be his fiancé, "I said, picking up an item from a box.

"Well I still say you should be the one with Romey. I don't know what I'm going to do with you girl. I can't believe that you left a jamming party to come home and unpack boxes."

"Well I've been busy Val and hadn't had time to finish unpacking."

"Yeah right — whatever Rach," Val said, eyeing me pathetically.

"I just can't seem to find a man who is on the same page with me," I whined.

"I think that Romey is on the same page as you are Rachel — what about him," Val said, in a teasing tone.

"Oh come on already Val! I told you a thousand times — Romey and I are only friends."

"Yeah, yeah, yeah — that's what you keep saying Rachel. But I'm just not convinced of that shit girl. Now you mean to tell me that you never thought about getting with Romey — not even once?"

"We've been over this Val! I told you — Romey and I have never been together like that!" I responded in an agitated tone.

"Okay — okay Rach. Take a chill pill girl. I'll let it rest for now, okay?"

I sighed and looked at Val, who was standing there with that silly smirk on her face. I thought to myself, *if she only knew how I really felt about Romey."*

Suddenly, I just remembered the invite that I had to Frannie's house get-together. Frannie had invited me when I was at the party.

"Oh — Val — I suppose to go to a party for Frannie. I don't know what to get her," I said, in a somewhat panicky voice.

"Do you want me to pick up something for you?" Val offered.

"Would you Val? That would really help me out."

"You know that I'll hook you up. But now — I got to go. I'll see you tomorrow," Val said, as she was headed out the door.

After Val had gone, I finished the rest of the unpacking. I was beat. It had been a very long night and I decided that I would go to bed. As I drifted off to sleep, I thought that tomorrow would be a new day, but for now, it was time for sleep.

Chapter 4

The next day when I arrived at Frannie's house for the shower, it was in full swing. There was a huge stack of gifts in the living room, to which I added mine. The ladies were just preparing to start a game when I walked in. The women all greeted me and asked me to join in. There were several platters of appetizers sitting on the table that didn't look all that special to me. In my opinion, they didn't look like much of an appetizer — little pieces of salami on small cracker squares. This really wasn't my cup of tea, but I decided to humor them and went along with everything, including these pitiful, little salami sandwiches. I don't know why these people had to try to be so ghetto with the food trays but I guess they were trying to save some money.

The women were all about to begin some type of a game that was similar to Jeopardy or Family Feud. I found out very quickly that these ladies knew next to nothing about having a good time. When the game started, I ended up answering most of the questions and got the evil eye for doing it. I couldn't help it that I knew most answers. Franchesca ended up asking me to give the others a chance, which was just her polite way of asking me not to play anymore. Her request was fine with me because I didn't want to play the stupid game anymore anyway.

Finally, the time came for Franchesca to open up her gifts. She really seemed to have fun with this because all of the gifts that she had opened so far were very nice ones. I decided to stay until she'd opened all of her gifts and then very tactfully invented an imaginary meeting that I had to get to. After hugging Frannie and wishing her well, I headed out the door.

As soon as I had left the shower, I phoned Romey and asked him if he would meet me at the park. I felt the urgent need to talk to him about his upcoming nuptials. My senses were literally screaming to me that Frannie was just not right for him. She was just too materialistic and I felt that she didn't love Romey for the right reasons and that all she wanted was the prestige she would get by being his wife.

Romey greeted me with that wonderful smile of his and gave me a warm hug. There was a hot dog stand nearby and he bought me my favorite, a polish sausage with lots of grilled onions and mustard. This was a welcome treat from the cucumber sandwiches they had at the shower. Romey got a regular hot dog with mustard and a couple of fountain drinks. We sat down on a park bench and ate while we chatted about things in general. But I really wanted to know more about Frannie — everything —about how and when the two of them met. I wanted to really know why he was going to marry her — I wanted to know it all. After all, Romey was my best friend and all I wanted for him was the best.

After finishing off our food, the two of us went for a stroll.

"So Romey — how did Franchesca and you meet?"

"Well — I was at an Old School Bash over in the Bronx and a mutual friend sort of hooked us up. The two of us kind of hit it off and we started going out. We seemed to just click together. Before I realized it, she and I were dating."

"So the two of you clicked huh?"

"Yeah — we clicked."

"Romey — she's not your usual type of woman."

"What do you mean by she's not my usual type Rach?"

"Well, you know what I'm talking about Roman Anthony Sinclair. Don't even try to play me like that," I said with a mock angry tone.

We looked at each other and then burst out into laughter.

"Yeah, yeah — I know what you're talking about. Truthfully, I don't know Rach — things just changed for me after I got older. You know I played the game for a while, but now, that kind of stuff no longer interests me. I want to settle down — and well — maybe I can do this with Frannie," He confessed humbly.

"But are you really sure about dating her seriously Romey? I mean — do you love her?"

"Yes – I think so Rach — maybe I do. She makes me feel like I have never felt. I've never felt this way about no other woman."

My heart silently sank; as I listened to Romey speak these wonderfully, moving words about this woman. I've never seen him so taken before so I guess this feeling that he has for Frannie is real. Though I secretly longed that he would see me this way, I forced myself to share in my best friend's happiness. I honestly did want him to be happy and it seemed as though he has found his happiness with Franchesca.

I reached out and hugged Romey tightly and wished him heartfelt happiness with Frannie.

"If Frannie makes you happy, then this is what I want for you too. So — when is the big day?"

"It will be one month from today. You are coming right? I got to have my best friend there."

"Sure Romey — of course I will be there."

Romey placed his arm around my shoulder and kissed me lightly on the cheek.

"Thanks Rach. Your being there will mean a lot to me."

"What are friends for," I replied with a smile, as we continued our walk in the park.

Today, I had an interview that my boss had asked me to set up with a rising, new female artist. Michael wanted me to do a story on a solo artist named *NADiA.* One of her albums that received rave reviews was called *"Reflections of NADiA, Soul of a Butterfly."* This was a very personal album and was comprised of many love ballads. The fans loved her.

I phoned *NADiA* and set up a time for an interview and we mutually agreed upon a time that would be satisfactory for both our schedules. We both decided on meeting at *Gallina's,* which was a unique, family owned and operated restaurant in Manhattan. It is nice to see the owners walking around the restaurant checking on customers. It gives the feeling of being at home. The food is out of this world; it is definitely one of the best in southern dining. The restaurant also had an intimate, garden atmosphere, appeal, and featured some of the best live R & B entertainment, dancing nightly, and could seat groups up to about 400.

I had arrived at the restaurant a little early as usual and the owner had taken me to a booth where I waited for *NADiA's* arrival.

When *NADiA* made it, we ordered some drinks; I got my favorite champagne cognac, Remy Martin XO, and she ordered Hennessy with ginger ale. After our drinks arrived, we began the interview.

"Rachel, you know it really kicks your butt sometimes," *NADiA* says, taking a sip of her drink and settling into the start of the interview.

"Yeah, I know that touring has to be tough on you," I added smiling attentively.

"You know Rachel, my boyfriend and I drove till four in the morning last night. We had an 8:15 wake-up call and got right back on the road again. I phoned you the minute I got into my room."

"*Nadia* — you are releasing your fourth solo album, "*I AM NADiA REED*", which is a mélange of soulful, melodic hooks, with a sweet, yet slightly husky R & B sensibility. Your first album is fully eligible for a Grammy nomination and it looks likely to grab a spot in the best new R & B category. So how do you feel about that?" I asked, before taking another sip of my cognac.

"I'm in an absolute tizzy of delight," *NADiA* said, beaming proudly of her accomplishments.

I learned from *NADiA* that the singer/songwriter started her musical journey 12 years ago as one half of a duo named "*THE AMAZON QUEENS*".

After family life became too overwhelming for her partner-in-song — her sister Kelli — *NADiA* went at it alone. Also, I learned that her surname is Reed and that she's on a perpetual tour, both throughout the U.S. and Internationally. Many of her songs deal with the aspects of love. I was very interested in what this young lady had to say because her life sounded so wonderful, so I continued with the interview.

"*NADiA* — I wanted to ask you a little bit about your past. How long did your sister and you make music together as *THE AMAZON QUEENS*?

NADiA smiled graciously and began speaking.

"Well, the two of us started *THE AMAZON QUEENS* in the later part of 1983. It was in August I remember", *NADiA* said, tracing a slender finger around the rim of her glass.

"We put out our first album in August of 1984. We toured first as a duo and then with a band until the birth of Kelli's first child, which was in February of 1990. So I would say we stayed together about six years. After the birth of her child, we continued to record as *THE AMAZON QUEENS*, and Kelli managed to tour with me through 1992. So it was really more like nine years. Shortly thereafter, I started singing solo."

NADiA paused momentarily, and then continued.

"At first, I kept touring as *THE AMAZON QUEENS* with the guys in the band. We kept it like that for a while, but something felt strange and somewhat out of sync. It felt like I was getting away from what the essence of the music was about. When you perform with a lot of people, there's a lot of logistical management, lots of craziness and stuff — I just kind of wanted to get back to my music and me. And that's what I did on my first solo album, *I'm For Real.*"

"Okay — now, after spending so many years working with your sister, did you find it difficult to set out on your own?" I asked.

"Yes it was — it was enormously difficult — on so many levels. Kelli was my business partner, so we made all of our business decisions together. She was my right arm and she was there when I messed up a lyric on stage. She was there to do ten million things. Generally, the way things worked was that Kelli was the liaison to the outside world — to the promoters or agents or whomever — and I basically would be sitting somewhere quiet working on being creative and writing songs. Kelli was the one who came up with the melodies for the songs that I wrote. So yes, I would have to say that it was really, really hard — because I lost so much when Kelli stopped singing with me. We are still very close and we speak on the phone a lot — especially right before I go on stage. Kelli and I do get to sing together, just not like it used to be."

"This newly released album, *"You Spoiled Me,"* actually kind of brings things full circle. We almost said that the album was by *THE AMAZON QUEENS* because five of the twelve tracks have Kelli and me harmonizing together. Harmony was a key part of *THE AMAZON QUEENS'* sound. But we mutually agreed that *THE AMAZON QUEENS* would not receive the credit for this album because Kelli could only join me at a small number of live performances," *NADiA* said, with a reserved feeling of sadness.

"All right *NADiA* — I think that I understand just where you are coming from. Now, correct me if I'm wrong, but I'm thinking that you didn't want to mislead anyone about your performances and your new album. Am I right?"

"Exactly," *NADiA* said, and nodding in agreement.

"Okay — Do you sense an appreciable difference between the work you produced as *THE AMAZON QUEENS* and the work that you create now?"

"I think that I have more maturity in my writing now. With so much music out there, your music has to stand out on its own. Your voice has to stand out on its own. So it has to go so much deeper," *NADiA* explained.

"Are there any R & B artists that you're particularly influenced by," I asked.

"Yes — I love Aretha Franklin. I feel enormously influenced by her in the sense that her songs were her ministries — and her voice was her temple. In my book, she definitely earned the title *"The Queen of Soul"* with her heavenly voice terrestrial passion. With 20 number one R & B hits and 17 Grammies, in my opinion, that was the thing that made her a monarch in music. Her title has never rung false and still holds up," *NADiA* spoke with much admiration.

"Okay *NADiA*— Why did you choose music as your form of expression?"

"I just love doing it. Also, I'm just a die-hard romantic. I found that through music I could express what I'm feeling. But reality is in the mix too — the reality that you have to eat and keep a roof over your head. Fortunately for me, I can do it doing something that I love — music."

"Are you surprised at how far your career has come? With two hit albums and a strong possibility for a music award nomination, do you reflect on your success?"

"Well — yes, I do reflect on my success. Every so often I will go, "Wow", I really like this place that I'm at right now. I'm really happy to be doing this and I quite often let out deep sighs of accomplishment. Sometimes everything just seems so unbelievable. My mind revisits the many places that I've been and I think of the successful albums that I've made. I secretly hope that there are many more albums to come and many more places to go."

All right *NADiA*, I have one last question for you. What's with the small (i) in your name?" I inquired.

NADiA laughs and repositions herself in the chair.

"You know other people have asked me that very question. You will probably think that my answer is odd too, but here it goes. This was the way I wrote my name when I first began writing. I think I was about five years old and I just continued writing it that way. My parents and my teachers tried to stop me from writing my name like that, but their suggestion never lasted for very long. I would just revert back to writing my name with a small (i). When I look at it now, it sort of seems like a neat logo or something."

"Now I think that's really is an interesting thing with the way that you do your name. I like it. I've had such a great time doing this interview with you and you're such a beautiful person. I wish you continued success with your music *NADiA*.

I turned off the tape recorder and smiled admirably at *NADiA*.

"Well, I guess that's a wrap and I want to thank you for your time."

"Oh no, the honor is mine. You're a great editor and a very well known one. You are so easy to talk to," *NADiA* replied.

"Thank you, but you made it very easy," I said modestly.

After finishing our drinks, we said our good-byes and went our separate ways. I headed back to the office contented in the fact that I had a great story and that Michael would be very pleased.

Chapter 5

It was a wonderfully sunny, May morning. I had gotten up bright and early and was ready to begin my day. My mind was on getting into the office and finding out what work Michael had lined up for me. I thoroughly enjoyed my job because I got to travel and meet so many different people. All of my interviews turned out very well and Michael says that I'm a natural at talking to people. He refers to the work that I do as *"top-notch"*, but I really just love the job.

As my day progressed, I found myself thinking of Romey and Franchesca. There was definitely something off about their relationship in my eyes. She seemed to want to mold and shape Romey into the man that she wanted him to be.

"Why couldn't she just love the man just as he is as I do", I mumbled.

Wow — I can't believe that I just said that out loud, I thought to myself. I guess that I'm finally admitting it to myself that I do love the man, but I just can't tell him that.

Letting him know that I love him would ruin our friendship and I will no longer have a best friend. So I will have to keep that information to myself and just ignore the surfacing feeling that I may have.

I've always believed that if you loved someone, you accept him or her as they are and for whom they are. Frannie didn't seem to share in his love for music. All she appears to see is the money and prestige that comes with big a big-time recruiter of recording artists. I suspect that Romey and Frannie will clash one day because of that very fact. But I do hope that for Romey's sake that the both of them can make it work together. I did want my best friend to be happy. And if Frannie makes him happy, then this is what I want too.

Romey and I have always shared our love of music. But Romey had a profession that I didn't really care for much because I felt it changed my best friend into being someone who was cold and calculating. The Romey who did this job was not the one I had known almost all my life. He was an executive at this land developing company. Romey's boss, Darren Waddell, is a real piece of work. He's the CEO of Waddell Land Developers and has no scruples when it comes to business. For Darren, acquiring real estate and property is strictly about money and he doesn't care how he has to get it. All Darren wants is to make money — at any cost. He doesn't take pride in moral issues as Romey does. With him, he will do anything as long as it makes him money. From what Romey has told me about him, I know it will be only a matter of time before the two of them parted company.

A knock on my office door broke my thoughts and in rushed a very elated Michael holding up a magazine and waving it in the air.

"Rachel — your article on *NADiA* was wonderful as always. Bringing you aboard was the smartest move I could have made. I'm working on getting you some more interviews. Keep up the magnificent job that you have been doing," Michael raved on his way back out the door.

After the long day at the office, it was so great to get home and relax. I had taken a long hot, relaxing shower and was walking about my apartment clad in nothing but my towel.

The doorbell rings and I walk over closer to the door and asks, "Who is it?" while glancing over at the wall clock.

"It's Romey Rach. May I come in?"

Nervously I looked down at myself and suddenly remembered that I was only wrapped in a towel. Then I thought, all hell, its only Romey. He could care less about how I looked and that I was wrapped in only a towel. Hesitantly, I decided to go ahead and open the door.

Romey walks in with an odd look on his face. I instinctively knew that something was on his mind and that he wanted to talk. He and I seemed to have had a sort of sixth sense about things like that and was right in our presumptions the majority of the time. Romey walks over to the sofa and seats himself and I followed and sat down beside him.

"You know Rach — Darren Waddell doesn't have any scruples. Small landowners should be protected from land-grabbing pigs like him, and they should be getting a fair price of their land. Darren has a section of unscrupulous people backed by high ups and a very powerful quarter of the government behind him. These people help Darren acquire property through manipulation of records and preparing fake deeds. I have morals Rachel and this type of stuff bothers me. At first, I could only see the big bucks that came with doing this job. Believe me; the job does pay me very well. But my conscious has started to bother me now and I have to do something. I can't go on like this."

Romey got up quickly from the sofa and began pacing about the room angrily. I got up and started to speak, but Romey broke in and interrupted me.

"You know, Darren angered me so damn much that I was just a fraction away from quitting the company. Then I got to thinking about the money I would be throwing away and the fine clothes that I can buy for myself and I just couldn't go through with it. I'm such a coward — I'm just a chump," he said with a pitiful look adorning his handsome face.

"You're neither a chump Romey nor a coward. Maybe it just isn't the right time for you to leave. Don't be so hard on yourself. When the time is right, you will know, okay?" I said gently touching his face.

I put my arms around Romey to console him and hugged him tightly. I felt so badly for his turmoil. It was as though I could feel his pain. I cradled his saddened face in my hands and kissed him lightly on the cheek. Romey now looked at me in such a way that it caused my heart to ache for him. As I looked into his soft brown eyes, all I wanted to do was to make things better for him. When I kissed him again, it was on his lips, which was followed by another kiss, then another. After the second kiss, Romey began to respond back and our kisses became deeper as we succumbed to the delightful surge of passion that was quickly rising between us. I got so caught up in the moment that my bath towel had fallen and my bare body was exposed. The airy feeling of my exposed body caused me to stop kissing Romey and made me realize what I was doing.

I quickly stepped away from Romey, embarrassed for kissing him the way that I did and also for my nudeness in front of him.

"I-I-I'm sorry Romey. I-I-I didn't mean to — you'd better go," I stammered, clutching my towel around me and dropping my head in total embarrassment.

"Yeah — yeah — you're right," Romey spoke huskily as he turned to walk away. He had made it almost to the door when a voice inside me told me to stop him.

"Wait Romey. Wait a minute."

Romey stops at the door, turns around, and walks back to where I was still standing.

"You will do the right thing about Darren. Just follow your heart okay?"

Romey stares at me seriously for a moment before breaking his stance.

"I'll see you later Rachel."

"Sure," I smiled weakly.

As I watched Romey go out the door, my heart sank. At that moment I realized and knew that I loved him, but I dare not speak those words out loud to anyone. For his sake, I had to keep our relationship plutonic. At least now I can acknowledge to myself that deep down I didn't love him as a friend, but as a woman would love her man. My heart knew now the revelation of my unsung love for Romey.

Chapter 6

Today had been a melancholy kind of day for me. I had gone through the motions of my job all day long and finally it was time to go home. I couldn't wait to hit the bath to try and release my tensed-up muscles.

The bath did help to relax me, but it didn't take away the thoughts of Romey. I tried watching T.V. and reading some magazines, but nothing seemed to work. My concentration was really off and nothing that I tried to do made sense. Since my body felt tired, I decided on going to bed.

In bed, I was a little restless because Romey was in my heart. I love him, but cannot allow the love that I feel for him to surface. Those feelings had to be kept dormant because I wanted him and Frannie to make a life together. Rather than mope about what I have lost, I reminisced about the fun times Romey and I have had over the years. Before long, I had drifted off in a calm, dream state and all was well again.

Saturday morning had arrived and I woke up feeling sorry for myself. I had also tried to get myself back on track, but nothing seemed to work for me. Somehow, I had to stop myself from dwelling on Romey's life.

On this particular Saturday morning, since I was down in the dumps I was going to just sleep in. I had no plans, so sleeping late sounded good to me. I partially opened one eye and peered at the clock on my nightstand. It said 7 a.m. I turned over pulled the covers over my head. Honestly, I just didn't want to get out of bed.

Suddenly, someone began constantly ringing my doorbell. The constant ringing was such an irritation that I simply couldn't ignore. Agitated, I threw the covers back, hopped out of bed, and stomped all the way to the door.

"Who is it," I yelled in an irritated tone.

When I looked through the peephole, it was none other than Val.

"Girl, open this door," she said in a mock angry tone.

When I opened the door, Val just stood there for a moment eyeing me in a methodical way.

"See — I knew you were holding up here in this apartment feeling sorry for yourself."

Val walked in past me, not waiting for me to invite her to come in. So I just closed the door and trailed behind her into the living room.

"Rachel, I got big plans for you today. First, you're going to get dressed, and then, we're going to go shopping."

"I don't really feel like going out today Val."

"Oh, you're going — if I have to dress you and drag your sorry butt out of here. So you see — you need to get with the program because I would hate to have to resort to such drastic measures, okay?"

"Oh, all right", I pouted. "It's no use arguing with you anyway."

"That's right — because you know I will dog you until you do."

Val was right about dogging me because she could be relentless when trying to accomplish her mission. Without any further delay, I showered and dressed and Val and I were off to the mall.

Once we were at the mall, we strolled down the sidewalk window-shopping. I still was holding on to some residual stubbornness so I just trailed behind Val sulking.

"Girl, you need to stop pouting and check out some of this stuff. They have a lot of sharp things in here. So get your butt in gear and get over here", Val remarked, in a slightly scolding tone.

"Look Rachel — you got to dress to impress. You got to start dressing sexier. You know — you got to dangle a little of the goods as bait and you can hook any man you want, girl."

"I'm not trying to hook a man and I don't want to Val."

"Well it never hurts to be prepared Rachel. You never know what might happen. Remember what I said — dangle a little of the goods."

"I think that you dangle enough for the both of us," I said sarcastically.

"Whatever Rachel — we are not leaving this mall without getting you some nice things, okay?"

After spending a little more time in the mall, I began to lighten up and started to get into the shopping spirit. I did end up actually finding and purchasing two nice dresses and matching pumps. Then I accessorized with matching purses and gold dangle earrings.

Later that evening, I thought about how childish I had acted with Val. All she was trying to do was to lift my spirits. She has an idea that I love Romey; she just hadn't gotten me to admit to it — yet. Since I won't admit to her how I really feel about him, she's been still playing matchmaker. I smiled to myself and remembered some of the foolish, but earnest things Val has done to try to help me. I knew that she meant well, but she still gets overzealous sometimes.

The ringing phone snapped me back from my reverie. It was my cousin Valerie Reed.

"Hey Rachel, what you doing?" Valerie said, when I answered the phone.

"I got us a couple of hotties lined up for tonight. They are taking us out to dinner and dancing."

"Val — I-I-I- don't know about this blind date thing. They never work out," I stammered.

"Oh it'll be fun Rachel. Come on. You need to get out of that apartment anyway. What do you have to lose?"

"Nothing I guess. But I do have to see Romey and Frannie get married at 3 o'clock because I did promise him that I would be there Val."

"Okay then — but be ready at 6 o'clock. We all will see you then."

After hanging up with Valerie, I began getting ready for Romey's wedding. I'd opted for one of the dresses that I had purchased at the mall today. The dress of choice was this lavender, form-fitting sheath that enhanced my ample bust line. I showered and changed and I was putting the finishing touches on my make-up when the doorbell rang. I gave myself a quick once over in the cheval mirror and I actually looked very nice. I stayed at the wedding for a few hours and went from there to meet Val for my blind date. Depression had kind of claimed my life after Romey's admission of love for Franchesca and I had cared very little about my appearances or much of anything else. Thanks to Val's persistence, I had decided not to live my life in the past and try to move forward.

When I stepped out of my car in the restaurant parking lot, Val eyed me surprisingly.

"You ready girl? You look really nice," she complimented.

"You look nice too Val. Let's go."

Later at the restaurant, I was impressed with the place. It was definitely a few steps above some of the places I'd gone to on former dates. I had actually allowed my self to have a little fun and enjoy decent conversation. My date's name was Brian and he was kind of cute, even intelligent. Usually Valerie's matchmaking efforts were fruitless and turned out awful because most of the guys were self-gratifying losers who thought that they were Gods' gift to women. It was for this very reason that I had chosen to stay away from the dating scene. After all, who needs this kind of grief?

Our dinner was very delicious which included: Rib eye - 10 oz. cut served with Herb Butter Garnished with Caramelized Shoe-String Onion, Mashed Potatoes, Pelligrino Sparkling Water, with dessert being their famous Bread Pudding with Rum Sauce.

When dinner was over, our dates took us to The Sugar Bar/Lounge/Restaurant. It was on a hidden street, just south of Soho, behind a pair of inconspicuous doors. Sugar threw a shamelessly fun party almost every night of the week. Somewhere between the specialty drinks, the DJs and the dancing, guests found themselves having a highly memorable evening. Sugar's trademark B-day parties generated a buzz that turned Sugar into one of the most sought after venues for hosting large parties and cozy dinners. The attitude at Sugar was warm and inviting: the aesthetic was 1950s Palm Springs, Danish Modern: the music was a masterful high-energy mix of everything from rock and roll, and eighties to hip hop, chill out, house, funk, and classics, and the vibe (most importantly) was fun and uninhibited. A perfectly sized bi-level bar, lounge and restaurant that held upwards of 300 people, Sugar was small enough to feel intimate and large enough to be intriguing and comfortable. A stunning floating bar, soaring ceilings, banquette lined sculpture walls, flattering dim lights and a state of the art sound system, and movie screen, created a visually stimulating party den.

At least our dates weren't cheap. The Sugar Lounge aimed to set high standards with excellent service, knowledgeable bar staff that can certainly mix a fine cocktail, along with cool décor and funky music. But, of course, with high standards come high prices and a severe door policy; so don't even venture to Deansgate without your platinum card and your latest finery.

I did loosen up some and allowed myself to have fun. I guess that it was the atmosphere and the dancing. At any rate, I did have a good time. I had such a good time that I had become tired.

After thanking Valerie for getting me out of my apartment, I thanked my date for a very nice time. He offered to take me home, but I politely declined and asked him to stay on and enjoy himself.

Later after getting home, I changed into my silk nighties and got ready for bed. Reflecting back on the events of the evening I'd just had, I smiled contently. The evening had not been half bad. When I allowed myself to loosen up, I actually enjoyed myself. This blind date that Valerie had set up wasn't quite so bad after all. As I curled up into my bed, peaceful thoughts swirled about in my head, lulling me into a contented, dreamless sleep.

Chapter 7

Two Months Later

As the months lumbered by, I had gained my momentum and was taking care of business again. My boss told me how proud of me he was for my hard work and dedication to my writing, research, and interviews. I was a little proud of myself because I had just about come out of my depression.

It had been a difficult time for me over the past months. Some of the days had been fairly decent and others had felt like torture. I had never dreamed that I would take Romey and Frannie getting together so hard. It seemed to take all that I had within me to get through the days sometimes and not experience overwhelming sadness and loneliness I'd felt. I have worked very hard to cope with everything and believe that I've made much progress.

Val wasn't much convinced of my accomplishment and still insists that I should have been the one who was with

Romey. He now belonged to someone else and I knew that I had to create a life for myself somehow.

This Monday morning at the office was extremely chaotic. Tina walked into my office with her arms full of paperwork. I had managed to get nearly all of the paperwork delegated out to other assistant editors except one.

"This guy says that he wouldn't interview with no one but you Rachel. I really tried — sorry," Tina said, as she turned and left.

I let out a huge sigh in disappointment because I didn't feel like doing an interview right now. But it seems that I will have to suck it up and do this one. Mr. Christopher Greene wants to be impossible, but I'm a professional. I can do it.

I gave Mr. Greene a call and confirmed our meeting for his interview for tomorrow afternoon. He told me that he looked forward to seeing me.

After getting off work, I took a longer route home so that I could begin unwinding from my hectic day at the office. I had also stopped by a park before going home. Riverside Park South retained the industrial flavor of the railroad yard once situated on its grounds. Angular paths, formed from the old concrete relieving platforms, evoke the railroad tracks. Abandoned ramps and piers, as well as a rusting gantry, are iconic reminders of times and technologies past. The park's design included athletic facilities as well as areas for quiet reflection. Three basketball courts, two handball courts, and a three-quarter-size soccer field invite athletes to hone their skills. A promontory, esplanade, and winding walkway welcomed visitors who wished to enjoy nature and experience river breezes. Built atop the remains of the original wooden shipping Pier 1 was a 715-foot long recreational pier. The river would surround visitors to the pier almost completely, experiencing a view of Manhattan once reserved for sailors.

I particularly enjoyed some of the areas for quiet reflection. Lying in the shadow of the West Side Highway were boardwalks that curled like ribbons and marsh grasses. The trees and the water and the grass — it was all kind of a balance of nature. As I strolled along the boardwalk and the winding walkways, I felt welcomed and I enjoyed nature and experienced the river's breezes. I remembered times back in the day when the east bank of the Hudson River was a nest of rotting railways and a haven for drug dealers and addicts. The riverfront was unsettling in the daylight and unsafe at night. Now the park was a beautiful place for whatever your fancy may be.

Later on after getting home, I felt so relaxed. The stroll in the park was just what I had needed. I ran a hot bath filled with scented, velvety soft water and bubbles and sank into until the water started to get cold. Then I jumped into a pair of satin pajamas and slid underneath the covers. I felt so good after my long bath that I drifted off into a serene, peaceful sleep.

The next day, it was lots of work as usual at the office. Michael came by to see if I was ready for my interview with Mr. Greene. Mr. Greene was a very successful businessman who heads and uprising Fortune 500 Company in Bronx, NY. He runs a very profitable pharmaceutical company. Mr. Greene had suggested that we did the interview over dinner at the Four Seasons restaurant, so I agreed.

I arrived at the Four Seasons a little bit early. Mr. Greene had made our reservations for 5 p.m. that evening. The maître-d informed me that Mr. Greene had not yet arrived, so I opted to be seated at the bar until he had arrived.

The bartender asked if I would like a drink, so I agreed to a Chardonnay. I loved the wine's aroma and sweet flavor and it was easy to drink, with its' fresh, fruit flavors of apple, pear, citrus and melon, leaving a lasting palate impression. As I sipped on the chardonnay, I reflected on the restaurant itself.

The Four Seasons I have learned has been synonymous with the power lunch for more than four decades. This place was where the high rollers broke bread and the meals and deals end devoured the sirloin. One gets to choose from two different settings: the legendary Grill Room, with its soaring ceiling, rosewood walls, leather banquettes and rippling curtains made of brass beads. Or one could choose the romantic Pool Room featuring a gurgling marble pool framed by illuminated trees.

The Four Seasons also had very distinguished entrees and specialties like lusty civet of wild boar with pappardelle, lentil and sausage soup, roast turbot with root vegetables, grilled tuna in pomegranate sauce, steaks, bison, and pheasant breast.

Mr. Greene finally arrives at the restaurant and apologizes earnestly for his lateness. He ordered me another chardonnay and ordered dinner for the both of us.

"Well — Mr. Greene. Are you ready to begin the interview?"

"Please — don't be so formal. Call me Christopher or Chris — whichever one that you prefer. And may I call you Rach?"

"How did you know my first name?"

"I make it a special point to find out the name of the very beautiful woman whom I admire so very much."

I felt the blood rise to my face, as I fought to overcome the overwhelming shyness that now swept through me. Chris was a very handsome man and many woman have tried to bag him, but without success. I even found myself drawn to him. I mean — what's not to like about him. He was very successful, a gentleman, and — did I say handsome.

"Sure — you may call me Rachel or Rach if you like," I said smiling, and gathering my composure.

"I think that I like the sound of Rach, but I also like Rachel too."

"Well — okay — let's get started then."

Chris and I laughed and talked about all sorts of things ranging from his childhood to what type of music he liked. The entire interview went very well — so well that it really didn't seem like an interview. And the meal had been so delicious.

After Chris and I had finished the interview and dinner, we stayed and chatted for a while. The evening had been so enjoyable. Looking across the table at Chris, I riveted all of the attention he so graciously splurged on me and it was obvious that he was attracted to me. The question was — should I continue to allow myself to feel and enjoy this attention? *I thought, could I allow myself to take pleasure in what this handsome man has to offer?* I really needed to go on with my life and get over this thing I have for Romey. Maybe Chris was just the man that I needed. Maybe he was just what the doctor ordered.

When I arrived at work the next morning, it was as though my office was a flower boutique. When I read the card that was attached to one of the vases, it said:

My Dearest Rachel,

Thanks for such a wonderful evening. You are such a beautiful woman. I sincerely hope that

*you will allow me to see you again. I will call
you very soon.*

*All my love
Chris*

I was absolutely elated at this attention that Chris was placing on me. It felt wonderful and made me feel so special. I smiled contently to myself, as I admired all of the beautiful flowers that surrounded me.

"What is all this," Romey said, entering my office. "Did someone die?"

"Oh — so we are being a comedian today uh," I spouted back sarcastically.

"For your information, these are from Christopher Greene. I interviewed him yesterday."

"You don't get flowers like this from people that you interview. You don't know anything about this man. Hell, you just met him. I think he's just trying to be a smooth player. I know because I'm a man. This Chris dude just wants to get into your —

"E-n-o-u-g-h Romey — that's enough. You don't know anything about this man either."

"All right woman — just calm down. I admit that I was a bit out of line and I apologize. Anyway — I came here to — well — I — I came here uh-h-h-h — well?

Romey's voice trailed off as he lowered his head and a saddened look washed over his face.

"Romey — sweetie — what's wrong?" I asked in a concerned tone.

Romey raises his head to face me, "Come on — let's go for a walk in the park."

I could see that something heavy was weighing on Romey's mind, so we headed for the park.

After getting there, we strolled down the winding walkways and reminisced about the music that we both loved so much, 70's Motown. We talked about our favorite songs and dances from back in the day. R & B was so much a part of us — almost like the air that we breathed. No matter how old you were, it seemed like everyone grew up listening to Motown. This type of music has always been a favorite of both Romey and me. Back in the day, "How Sweet It Is," "Ain't Too Proud To Beg," "I Heard It Through The Grapevine," and "What's Going On," were just a few of these timeless classics that we both loved. Often referred to as the "Motown Sound," these classics were strongly rhythmic, had powerful bass lines, and were influenced by gospel.

"Romey — do you remember *"Rock Your Baby"* by George McCrae?"

"Yeah — yeah I do. I liked that cut."

We both looked at each other with a glint in our eyes and smiled profusely. We both knew what the other was thinking. Then Romey and I started singing harmoniously and swinging our heads back and forth to our own groove.

Woman, take me in your arms, Rock your baby. Woman, take me in your arms

Rock your baby. There's nothin' to it, just say you wanna do it. Open up your heart, and let the lovin' start. Woman, take me in your arms, Rock your baby. Woman, take me in your arms, Rock your baby.

Romey and I laughed and caught each other eyes, but it was fun and seemed to lighten his mood.

I cleared my voice and placed my hand on his, "You know Romey, I still think that you should try to record you a song. Your voice is so wonderful and I know other people would love it just as much as I do."

"Oh Rach — I don't know about that. I might not be any good."

"Just give it a try. You never know what may happen. Just give it one try, please — pretty please," I said, playfully pouting.

"I have written a few songs. I guess it wouldn't hurt to give it a try. Besides, you will probably dog me forever if I don't."

"You damn right I will dog you. You are really good Romey. So give others a chance to hear what I hear, okay? And I will be more than happy to do a write-up on you in the magazine."

"Sure Rach — anything for you. You know you my girl."

"Hey — what about this song Romey, do you remember *"Rockin Chair" by Gwen McCrae?"*

I started singing and Romey joined right in on cue.

Sexy baby, good lovin' daddy, Ooh, let me be your rockin' chair. Just-a rock me way from here. Let's get it on, come to me baby. Ooh, let me be your rockin' chair.

Just-a rock me way from here. Let your arms, shelter me from all hurt and pain

Mmm, light my heart, with your everlasting flame. Ooh, mmm-mmm. Sexy baby, (rock, rock) good lovin' daddy (rock, rock). Ooh, let me be your (rock, rock) rockin' chair. Rock (rock, rock) me way from here. Let's get it on (rock, rock), mmm, come to me baby (rock, rock). Ooh, let me be your rockin' (rock, rock) chair. Just-a rock (rock, rock) me way from here.

"See, that's why I'm not going to quit my day job and won't be pursuing a singing career," I said jokingly. "But you can my friend."

Then both Romey and I burst into laughter. We enjoyed kidding around with each other. We have always done silly stuff like that and laughed until our sides hurt at how funny we were. But Romey still sings to me on my birthday and I guess he always will. I hope that by his marrying Frannie, that it would not change this part of our friendship.

Chapter 8

Sunday morning, several weeks after my first encounter with Chris, I drove out to Central Park and sat on a bench beside the lake. The strong breeze rippled the quiet water, and I closed my eyes, held my face up to the sun and breathed deeply of the clean fresh air. I had a decision to make and sought the peaceful surroundings to help me clear my head and focus on the pros and cons of an important step I would likely take. Chris wanted to date me seriously and see where the relationship will take us. I smiled contently as I thought of how divinely delicious Chris was. He had so much going for him: looks, charm, status, prestige, tenderness, caring, stability and sex appeal. There was a possible chance that abiding love could come from this relationship if I gave in to it and allowed myself to feel. After some deliberation, I decided that I would give Chris and me a chance and see where it goes.

After getting home, I phoned Chris and shared with him my decision to date only him exclusively. He was absolutely elated about the chance to be with me and started right away making plans for our next reunion.

It was Monday morning and I was back in the office working on various articles. Michael entered my office and told me that he had lined up another interview for me with an important CEO of a major law firm. After going over the details with me, he disappeared down the hallway. Since this interview was a few weeks away, I had sufficient time to prepare and be on top of my game. I could now turn my attention to non-mundane things and work more relaxed for a while instead of having to worry about deadlines. This hassle-free time also gave me an opportunity to daydream about Chris. He was a wonderful man to be with and I always have a great time when we are together. The two of us actually had a real shot at having a relationship if I didn't mess it up. I was determined to make a go of it because I wanted to get on with my life have that special someone to spend quality time with at the end of the day.

My ringing phone interrupted my daydreams.

"Hello — This is Rachel Pendleton — how can I help you?" I spoke into the receiver kindly.

"What's up girl — It's Romey," he said in an edgy tone. "Can you get away from the office for a bit? I really need to talk."

"Sure Romey — Can you give me a minute? I'll meet you at the park in say, a half hour?"

"Hey, that will be good. I will see you then."

I called Michael up and told him that I would be out of the office for a little while and that I had an important errand to run. I gathered up some files that I needed some additional information on and asked Tina to take care of that for me.

"I'll get right on it Rachel and will leave them on your desk, okay?"

"That would be great Tina and I will be back shortly," I said on my way out the door.

On the drive to the park I wondered what was wrong with Romey because I could sense it in his voice on the phone. I hoped that Frannie had not done anything to hurt him. I knew that Romey loved her, but she was such a selfish, self-serving individual. She always has to have things her way and really don't consider the feelings of her husband very much.

After arriving at the park, I parked my car, and headed for the area of the park where Romey and I usually hung out. Shortly, I spotted him leaning back against a large magnolia near the lake with one foot up on the tree.

"What's wrong Romey," I said in a concerned tone, as I approached him.

"Let's take a stroll while we talk, okay?"

"You remember that Luther Vandross song, *"It's Hard for Me to Say,"*

Then Romey started to sing it to me in a robust, ardent tone. *"Didn't know 'til today, That you would love for me to say, All of things I feel, Though you don't doubt they're real, Insecure, very shy, Are the only reasons I have why, I never say the things that you would love to hear, All the words I try, Disappoint me and I cry, So they're words I don't always say."*

"Oh-h-h-h! What you do to me with your singing. You sing so damn good Romey," I spurted out admirably.

"I wanted you to know that I heard you when you told me that I should cut a demo of some of my songs. I believe in what you think and I trust you Rach because you have always been in corner. I've decided that I will do the demo and see what happens."

At that very moment, I suddenly threw my arms around Romey like a circle around the sun. *Gosh this man smelled so good I thought to myself.* Then reality abruptly struck a cord in me and I came to realize what I was doing.

"That's great news Romey," I said, releasing my claim on him. "So — when are you going to do the demo?"

"I don't know — but it will be soon, okay?"

"Good — that's good," I said, nodding in agreement.

"I just have one teeny little problem. I've got to tell Frannie. She isn't going to like it because she thinks that I will never be able to make it as a singer/songwriter. She just doesn't believe in me like you do Rach. She loves this job that I do. You know — it brings in the big bucks."

"Well Romey, just try to talk it over with her. She may surprise you."

"You really think that she will understand Rach?"

"Sure I do. I support you and she will too," I said, trying to look confident.

"Thanks for always being there for me."

"You know I will always be here for Romey. You're my boy — my best friend," I said, gathering his hands into mine.

Romey and I began slowly walking, while holding hands. Anyone who saw the two of us would have thought that we were lovers. As we walked, my eyes admiringly swept over his handsome face. *I wondered what it would be like to be in an intimate, loving relationship with him. I wondered how it would feel to be physically loved by this man — to be held, caressed, and deeply and passionately kissed by this man.* Then reality quickly jolted me back to the here and now. *Oh — my — God I thought. What the hell was I thinking? Get a grip Rachel Pendleton. This man is married and you have just decided to pursue a new relationship with Chris.* I quickly shifted gears in my mind to some safer thoughts.

"Hey — look — uh-h-h — I got to get back to work. Remember what I said — Give Frannie a chance. Tell her about your decision to make a demo. If she loves you, she will support you, okay?"

"Alright Rach — I'll catch you later."

Romey and I said our goodbyes and I headed back for the office. When I arrived at the office, Tina told me that she had left a message on my desk and that she had gotten all the information ready for me that I needed in order for me to finish my work. My message was from Chris and he wanted me to call him. So I did just that — I called.

"Hello — This is Christopher Greene. How can I help you?" he said, his sexy voice echoing through the phone.

"Hi Chris — This is Rachel. I was just returning your call."

"Well hello beautiful. How are you this wonderfully gorgeous day?"

"I'm doing great and you?"

"Oh I'm doing just terrific now that you called. I was wondering if you would be interested in a dinner date tonight. I promise that I won't keep you to late."

"Chris, I was planning on doing some writing tonight to prepare for an upcoming interview."

"Tell you what — come on over to the penthouse after work and bring your notes with you. You can work while

I prepare our meal. How is that? I'll even help you if you want."

"Well –l-l-l-l, I don't know. You may be a distraction."

"Okay — how about this? I promise to be on my best behavior, okay?"

"Alright Chris — you win. I give in. I will come. I'll be there around 6 o'clock, okay?"

"Okay sweetness. I'll be waiting."

After hanging up the phone, I sat there smiling contently to myself. I felt certain that Chris would do his best to give me time to work while I was at his penthouse. From what I've seen so far, he has been a man of his word. It is such a nice change of pace having someone cook for you — especially when you are used to picking up some takeout from the Chinese restaurant.

I did manage to get back to work and finish the rest of my day, though thoughts of Chris would occupy my mind from time to time. I had such a great time on our previous date and it made me want more. I wondered if he could be the one who could get me over Romey. Could I possibly have a real relationship with him?

After work, I was at Chris's penthouse by 6 o'clock as planned. He greeted me at the door with a warm hug and a gentle kiss on the cheek.

"Come in Rachel — welcome to my home," he said politely.

When I walked through the door, I was in awe at the appearance of his penthouse. It was very beautiful and spacious and I could see how he could be very comfortable here. The penthouse had cachet — with a broad, spectacular view of Manhattan's Fifth Avenue and the wide acres of Central Park.

"Your penthouse is so beautiful Chris."

"Thank you my dear — it is pretty comfortable to me"

Chris took me by the hand and led me to the study of his home. It was amazing too because it looked like a miniature library complete with a striking cherry oak office desk and computer.

"Here is where you will be able to work undisturbed until our dinner is ready Rachel," he said, pulling back the high-back black leather executive chair.

"Have a seat here sweetie and you can get started on your work."

I made myself comfortable at the desk as my eyes admiringly swept over the room. I had been used to sitting on my couch on crossed legs working with my paperwork scattered all about, but this was much nicer.

"I will be back later to check on you Rachel," Chris said smiling brilliantly as he was leaving the room.

Chris checked on me now again to make sure everything was all right and to see if I needed anything. After about an hour and a half he came to get me for dinner. I gathered my paperwork together, put all of it in my folder, and followed Chris to the dining room.

The dining room was luminescent and set so beautifully with candelabras and flower bouquets. This room was all about light, with huge windows and lots of wide-open light-drenched space. There was a magnificent Versailles crystal chandelier hanging above the dining table. I liked the airy quality of the framework and the way light danced off the beveled edges of the crystal pendeloques. There was also a bottle of wine chilling on the table.

Chris's kitchen was a high-tech kitchen with all of the gadgets. There were four pendants that hung over a luxurious bar that were made of what seemed to be parallelograms of densely woven Strass crystal. Pure white halogen light ignited the crystal to create shimmering auras of color. It was absolutely beautiful.

"Have a seat beautiful," Chris said, seating me at the table.

"I adore cooking and I hope that you enjoy the meal that I have prepared for us."

"I'm sure that I will — everything smells great."

Chris and I laughed and talked all through dinner. He was such a gracious host and a wonderful cook. The meal he had prepared was delicious.

After dinner, Chris and I went for a stroll. His penthouse just happened to be located near some ideal spots for smooching. Some the most accomplished Casanovas know that a truly unforgettable kiss requires far more than extraordinary techniques and expert timing. In order to weaken a loved one's knees in one fell smooch will take something else as well as a well-scintillating location. It would be hard to beat that southern road with the flamingo orange backdrop where Clark Gable finally locked lips with Vivian Leigh in *"Gone with the Wind."* Here in New York, there is no real reason for not being able to get it right. Experienced New Yorkers know that there are dozens of spots just crying out to be the setting for an awe-inspiring kiss. It's just a question of finding the right one. New York is one of the most romantic cities in the world if you know where to go.

A few sights that I know of as enchanted locales for smooching are Manhattan's own Central Park. Morning, afternoon, or evening, the park's countless fields and benches are occupied by nuzzling lovers. It's a place where you can be quiet in the chaos of New York and share that with someone else.

Next on my list is the Brooklyn Bridge, reaching nearly 300 feet into the sky. It's more than just a vital link between Brooklyn and Manhattan, but it's a world-class make out spot. The bridge's expansive views across the East River can make even the coldest fish feel dreTina. Plus, bridges can be so romantic anyway because they're overlooking the world.

Another hotspot for lovers is the Cloisters Museum. It is a castle-like building in Fert Tryon Park and is an ideal place to sweep a new flame of their feet. Strolling hand in hand through tapestry-lined passageways is just what a couple would need for a little inspiration. Just a walk through would soften even the hardest nut.

Last but certainly not the least place for romance is Battery Park Promenade, which hugs the southern tip of Manhattan. For the lovebirds in search of privacy amidst natural splendor, there's no place better than this park. Couples can sit alone in a vast open space with panoramic views over the Hudson River.

Chris had selected Central Park as the place for our stroll. As we walked arm in arm down the walkways, a delicate breeze stirred, causing the curls tendrils across my face gently rise and fall. Chris made me laugh and I found myself becoming more and more enthralled by his charm and good looks. Our pace was slow and easy as we cruised down the winding passageways. Occasionally, I would lay my head on his shoulders and revel in his overpowering masculine smell. In the distance, I could hear the 'clap, clap, clap' of horses hooves that pulled a carriage with a couple nuzzled together.

Chris and I were really enjoying each other's company until suddenly he just stopped walking. His abrupt stop caused me to slightly step away from him and look at him in surprise.

"What's wrong Chris? Is something wrong?" I asked in wide-eyed astonishment.

"Oh no baby — there's nothing wrong. I'm sorry for surprising you that way. I just wanted to admire your beauty," he said apologetically.

He paused briefly and then continued.

"You know Rachel — you are a very beautiful woman."

Chris's comment had me blush and I could only look at him in wide-eyed bafflement and try to cover the shy feeling that now washed over me. I simply couldn't allow him to sense that his comment had such a profound effect on me, so I had to come back with something.

"Yeah - right. So you think I'm beautiful uh?" I responded, trying to appear unmoved by his comment.

"Yes Rachel– I do think that you are beautiful. What's wrong with that sweetheart?' he asked calmly.

I stood and stared at Chris, trying to look as though his words had been ineffective. But I knew that deep down inside I tingled all over at the mere thought of his words.

"So-o-o-o — answer this question for me Chris. Do you think that you are going to get you some booty tonight?"

"Yes I do think that will happen — at some point, but not tonight. I feel that it will happen in due time. All I have to do is be a patient man," he said with a mischievous wink.

"Hey — you know what? You are just a tad bit conceited. You think that you got all the right moves to sweep a woman off her feet don't you? And — you are awfully sure of yourself aren't you?"

"I believe that I will be around for a while and think that my chances are actually pretty darn good."

"Oh-h-h — you think so do you?

I turned to step away. To my surprise, Chris grabbed me, quickly pulled me into his arms, and planted the hottest, smoldering kiss on me. In the beginning, I was slow to respond to his kiss. But his kiss was so sweet and urgent. Before I realized it, I had unconsciously put my arms around him and had parted my lips for a deeper passionate kiss. Heat plowed through me, as I braced myself against him and fully surrendered my mouth to him willingly.

When Chris finally released me, I was almost breathless and felt almost dizzy from our kiss. I could only gaze into his dark brown eyes in a helpless bewildered state.

"So-o-o-o — tell me Rachel— what do you think of that move?"

"Well Chris — I'll tell you what — it's like what you say to chef at a very nice restaurant about dessert — It was delicious — I would like seconds please."

Chris and I embarked upon another fiery, passionate kiss. This time, the kiss we shared was equally responsive. As I melted back into Chris' arms and settled in for another sensual kiss, my world felt alright. I felt that he could be the one that I could make a new life with and that I finally have a special someone in my life.

Chapter

9

I was in high spirits today. The prospect of possibly having a real relationship with Chris had lifted me to a new level in my life. I was treading in uncharted territory with Chris because the bulk of many of my relationships never reached that point. It felt wonderful having these developing feelings for this man and now they were penetrating my heart. The feelings somewhat mimicked the ones that I've felt for Romey over the years. The difference between the new feelings and the old was that the old ones were familiar and comfortable and the new feelings were starting to become special but were so tentative. As uncertain as I felt about Chris and me, I honestly wanted to give this new relationship a chance. After all, who knows — he may end up being the one.

On my drive into the office, I admired the beautiful day. I'd made my usual stop at the coffee shop and got coffee and donuts that I shared with the other members of the office staff. Michael was often away from the office or came in much later, but that was his routine and we all accepted it. I understood that Michael was president and CEO, but he seemed to be out a bit much to me. But he never failed to remind me of how fortunate he was to have me aboard and that he had complete confidence in me. I believe his exact words were "this place runs like a well–oiled machine when I'm away. I have no worries about the magazine because you practically run the place in my absence."

Michael's unwavering belief in me always lifted my confidence and he knew that I would never disappoint him. He trusted my judgment and any decision that I made for the magazine. I really felt as though he was grooming me for something more within the hierarchy of the company. I also had the respect of the entire office staff.

After seating myself at the desk, I slowly reclined in my chair allowing my thoughts to consume me. Life was good for me right now. I leaned forward and picked up a photo of Chris and me that I had on my desk. We had taken the photo soon after our first date and he had it framed for me. Chris was really a handsome man and had been one of the most sought after bachelors here in Manhattan. All of that had changed according to him, when I entered into his life. He certainly doesn't hesitate telling the single ladies that he is taken and that they should look elsewhere for a man. A smiled adorned my face as I admired the photo and I thought of how happy I feel now.

Light tapping on my door intruded my thoughts and then Michael entered the room.

"How are you this morning, Rachael?"

"I'm great Michael and how are you," I said putting the photo back in its place.

"I'm just wonderful my dear — just wonderful. Thought that I would check in with you before going to my office. I'm sure that everything is okay."

"Oh yes — sure. Everything is fine, but I would like to go over a new idea that I have and some projections that I've been working on about enhancing our advertising."

"Sure thing Rachel. I can't wait. You know — you have such great instincts that I totally trust. I have so much confidence in your abilities that I would like to make you an offer."

"An offer? What do you mean Michael by make me an offer?"

"Rachael — you have been like my right arm since coming to work for me. Hell — you practically run the place when I'm out of the office or away on business. You are a momuable asset to this magazine and you should be rewarded. With that being said, I would like to offer you the position of Editor and Chief of this magazine and I do hope that you will accept the position."

"Oh – my – God! Are you serious Michael? I mean — this is such a wonderful opportunity," I said trying to maintain my composure.

"I am positive that you are the right woman for the job, so all you have to do is say yes."

I quickly rose from my chair and extended my hand to Michael and let out an astounding, "Yes – oh yes. I'm honored."

"Great — wonderful. Then it's done deal," Michael said, shaking my hand vigorously.

"Rachael — I will be in my office for a few hours and then I have a business meeting to go to in Philadelphia. I know that I'll be leaving the magazine in capable hands. In the event that you do happen to need me for anything, you know how to reach me, okay?"

"Oh yes — sure Michael — and thank you for this opportunity."

"Oh no — thank you," Michael said on his way out the door.

I dropped back in my chair, spun it around, reclined back and stared out of my office window. *What a great opportunity I had just been given I thought to myself. Girl, your professional life is all falling in place and your love life is improving greatly. So why can't I have it all — love and career. It could happen. But a part of me is reluctant to accept so many good things happening in my life. That part of me is afraid because it feels that with so many good things happening, something bad is bound to come to pass. Then the strongest part of my inner self says, Girl — pay those thoughts no mind — you deserve this. You can have it all and be happy. You worked hard and you earned this promotion. As for your love life — well — you just need to sort through your feelings and decide whether or not you should tell Romey that you are in love with him.*

My ringing phone startled me and brought me back from my reverie. I quickly dismissed my last thoughts and answered the phone.

"What's up Rach!" a soft baritone voice echoed through the line.

"Hi Romey, what's going on?"

"Rach — a friend of mine is suppose to have my demo ready today and I want you to hear it, okay?"

"Sure Romey. I'm already excited just thinking about it. I know that it will be great. I'm so thrilled for you. Tell me — have you talked to Frannie yet?"

"No — I am going to tell her about my demo tonight. I already know that she won't approve of it."

Hey — remember what I told you Romey. Give her a chance. She may come around because she loves you."

"I wish Frannie was as easy to talk to as you are Rachael. That woman is probably going to split her wig over this."

"Listen to me Romey. All I ask is that you give her a chance. She may surprise you."

"Well — I don't know about that but I am going to try to talk to her about it."

"It'll be alright Romey. You'll see. Hey — guess what? I got a promotion. You are now talking to the new Editor and Chief of Sunrise Magazine."

"Oh yeah — see that's what I'm talking about, girl," Romey said giving me a high five. Michael finally recognized just how great you are. I knew it would just be a matter of time, Rach. I'm so happy for you. You know what? We need to celebrate when you get off work. We can go to River Café and get our drink on. You know — I believe they have a live band there tonight and we can get our groove on. You know how we use to do the damn thang — old school style ba-by!"

"Whoa-a-a Romey — slow down. We can't do that. You need to go home and talk to Frannie and I have a date with Chris."

"Damn — I'm sorry Rachael. I don't know what I was thinking. I just got so excited and carried away about your promotion. I'm just so damn proud of you. Look — Rach, this is a well-deserved promotion for you. Maybe we can do this another time, alright?"

"Sure Romey —maybe we can sometime."

For a moment the quietness between us was like a dead calm. I really didn't know how to dismiss the flushing feeling that was consuming Romey and me and I didn't speak a word. Both of us were uncomfortable and didn't know what else to say to each other. So I decided to break this overwhelming silence.

"Hey — Romey — look— I really need to get back to work. So I -- I'll talk to you later, okay?" I stammered.

"Yeah — yeah – uh – uh okay — right – alright then. Uh – take care. See you."

"Goodbye Romey," I said, placing the phone back into its cradle.

I sat there for a moment just reflecting on the conversation I had just had with Romey. I could not believe that I had lied to him about having a date with Chris. But I needed to try to set some boundaries for my relationship with Romey. After all, he is married and I have a relationship of my own with Chris. He and I running around together so much can't look very good given both our situations. I want to give him a chance to connect with Frannie as the person he talks to about important issues in his life — she is his wife for God's sake. But by the same token, I want to also give Chris and me a fair chance. I felt that this close connection of ours needs to be refined so that neither one of us will not be so dependent on the other. I must do the right thing to give both of us a chance to make our individual relationships work. The only way that I know how to deal with all of this is to put some space between us.

Chapter

10

Over the next several months, Chris and I seemed to be getting our relationship tighter. We seemed to be connecting on many levels and spent much our time together going to art shows, museums, going on boat rides, and whatever else that suited our fancy. Chris enjoyed cooking for me and spoiled me immensely. I took pleasure in all of the attention that he splurged upon me — all of the pampering and fussing over me was wonderful. I wasn't used to this kind of treatment from a man because most of the time they were never around long enough for it to matter. If Chris wasn't cooking specialty meals for me, he was wining and dining me in very nice restaurants. When I got off work, I went straight to his penthouse. Chris had a room he had set up especially for me to work in with a computer, fax, and printer. He wanted me to have the space to work and the tools necessary to work on my articles without him being too overbearing, yet he was available to be attentive whenever I needed him. Chris was always a welcome distraction when I was working because writing can be tiresome and challenging. Sometimes Chris would come into the room just to let me taste test something he's preparing for us. When he turned to leave, I would playfully slap him on the butt. Our relationship was doing very well and my feeling for him had greatly deepened over the past months.

I sometimes had idle time, which was a rare luxury in my line of work, but it allowed me time to reflect. After all of the months that had pasted, my mind had somehow drifted to Romey. I wondered how he was and if he and Franchesca had connected as Chris and I had. I had secretly hoped that our separation would enable relationship with Franchesca to connect on a level that was similar to the friendship he and I had.

Today had been a kind of slow day at the magazine. It had been a long time since I'd heard from Romey. I still hoped that his life was going well and I wanted so much for him to be happy because I had been so happy with Chris. My life was going great for once and I did wish the same for him. All that I have ever wanted for my best friend was for him to be happy — love and happiness. Franchesca could be good for him if she would stop being so self-indulgent. She was a nice enough person, but seemed to not allow Romey to be himself.

My ringing phone invaded my thoughts and brought me back to the here and now.

"What's up Rach," the familiar voice echoed through the line.

"Romey — Hi — I was just thinking about you," I said excitedly.

I could always tell when something was wrong with Romey by his brief silence after he calls me. He would always pause before he came out with whatever was troubling him.

"Uh — Rach — I —I kinda need to see you. I know we are not supposed to bother each other with our problems, but I have no one else that I can turn to right now."

Something was off with the tone of Romey's voice. He sounded so distant and bereaved. My gut feeling was telling me it had something to do with Franchesca.

"What's wrong Romey," I asked genuinely concerned.

"Want to go to lunch with me today? If you're too busy, I'll understand."

"No Romey — I'm not too busy if you really need to talk okay? You know I'm here and I'm your friend."

"I know Rach — you always are there for me. I do need to talk — so uh — what time and where do you want to meet?"

The park is good Romey and we can grab a couple of hot dogs or something."

"Yeah — you know — It's a guy out at the park who has a hotdog stand that sells some pretty great hotdogs. They're similar to the ones back in Chicago. You remember Rach — The Demon Dog? Back in the day, we used to woof down so many of those hotdogs."

"Yes — I remember. I think quite possibly those hotdogs were the best hot dog in the city. The prices couldn't be beat. I believe they cost around $2 for both hotdog and fries. The Demon Dog stand was always so crowded, but the service was fast. And who could forget all of the fun decorations and memorabilia?" I added. "I hear the stand is closed down now, but I really hope that the place will resurface again — it was fantastic! They really were a classic Chicago Hot Dog stand that made real Chicago style hot dogs. Man those were some kick ass hot dogs."

Okay Romey — let's do the demon dogs then. Give me about an hour, okay?"

"That will work for me. I'll see you at the park in about an hour."

After hanging up with Romey, I looked over some files that I had on my desk to see if any of them needed my immediate attention. There was nothing there that I could see that was so pressing that I had to deal with it at this present time.

As I was making preparations to leave, Tina softly knocked on my door and entered my office.

"Rachel — a representative of Harvey Stearns wants to know if you were the one who would do the interview with him."

"Oh no Tina. Tell Brian to do that one, okay?"

"Sure Rachel — I'll let him know."

"Uh — Tina — before you go — I will be out of the office for about an hour and a half for lunch today. If you need anything before I return, just give me a call on my cell, okay? Thanks." I said with a smile.

"We'll do Rachel. Have a good lunch." Tina said with a warm smile as she left my office.

When I arrived at the park, Romey was already there sitting a short ways from the hotdog stand. He was so absorbed in thought that he didn't even notice as I approached.

"Hey Romey" I said extending my arms to give him a hug.

"I apologize for not noticing that you had arrived Rach. My mind had just wandered off for a minute."

Don't even sweat it Romey. We're good."

Oh, I'm buying the hotdogs today," he said on his way to the stand.

I went and seated myself on the bench and speculated about what could be troubling Romey. It's probably a good guess that it is Franchesca. But I wondered what had she done this time.

Romey returned with hotdogs, fries, and two colas in a tray and seated himself next to me on the bench.

"Rach — you know earlier — my mind had kind of wandered off a ways and I just didn't see you coming," he stammered, showing genuine empathy as he handed me a cola.

"I noticed that Romey. So — What's got you so down? I can see that something is weighing heavily on your mind."

"Well Rachel — you know — I have been trying to talk to Franchesca about my wanting to quit my job and sing, but she is just bouncing off the wall. She's furious as hell with me."

"Did you finally tell her about the demo?"

"Yes I did — And I also tried to tell her about my quitting Waddell Land Developers.

"Wait – wait. You mean you actually left Darren Waddell's sorry ass?"

"Yeah — I mean — I just couldn't stomach doing that job anymore. That man has some serious issues. I'm tired of all the dishonesty, double-crossing, and cheating honest, hard-working people out of their property. It's good money and all, but I have a conscious. It really bothers me to see how unprincipled, deceitful, and immoral Darren has been. He never listens to nothing I have to say — especially when

I'm in his face about how he should try to be honest in his business dealings. Do you think that I'm wrong for quitting Rach."

"Of course not — you know how I felt about that job of yours. I think it's great that you are quitting because that job wasn't really for you anyway. You are a much better man than that Romey."

"I don't know how I'm going to be able to get through to Frannie. She's going to throw a hissy fit about this I just know it."

"Maybe not Romey. Just go home and try to talk it through. Talk to her just like you're talking to me."

"Oh alright — I will try, but she won't go for it.

I gave Romey a big hug and sent him on his way. Maybe he and Franchesca can work through this somehow. I certainly hope so for Romey's sake.

Chapter 11

It was a glorious day today. The sky was a gorgeous shade of blue and there was a breeze chasing through the red maple trees outside my apartment. I was in good spirits as I drove to my office this morning. Though my job would sometimes be demanding, I still loved it.

After getting to the office, I started making calls and setting up some interviews with some prominent movers and shakers in Manhattan which the preliminary interview work-up had already been done. A commotion outside the office suddenly pulled my attention from my work. When I looked out of my office window, I saw four suited individuals and three NYPD officers go into Michael's office. As they closed the door behind them, all of us in the office watched in awe. I stood in my office doorway and listened in disbelief, as the men's voices seemed to escalate in their tones. Within a few minutes, Michael's door opened and he was being escorted out in handcuffs by two of the suited men that turned out to be FBI agents. The other agents followed closely behind as did the NYPD policemen. I rushed toward Michael to try to find out what was going on.

"What's going on," I asked innocently.

Michael looked at me in a forlorn sort of way, but dropped his head without saying a word.

"Michael — where are these people taking you?"

Michael wouldn't even look at me. He just kept his head lowered and never attempted to answer.

"Why are you taking Michael away? There must be some mistake. What do you think he did?"

"Ma'am — Michael is being arrested for fraud, conspiracy, insider trading, and making false statements. He's been under surveillance for the past four years."

Oh – my – gosh – Michael is – this true? Please tell me that you didn't do what they are accusing you of. Michael — you look at me and tell me that this isn't true," I demanded angrily, as I lifted Michael's chin up to my face level.

Michael' eyes fell from mine as his guilt would not allow him to maintain direct eye contact.

"I'm so sorry Rachel," he finally managed to mumble out. "I'm so terribly sorry."

The agents led Michael away. As I watched them place him in their car, my heart sank and my stomach felt sick. My mind just couldn't comprehend what just happened here today. My boss had just been arrested by the FBI and led out like a common criminal.

The rest of my day went by in a blur. My concentration had been lost and I got very little work accomplished. Usually, I worked until late, but had decided to call it a day at three p.m. I had told everyone else that they could go home earlier. For the longest time I just sat at my desk in the office with my face furrowed in concentration on the astonishing events of today. I didn't know what would happen to the company. Maybe there will be no company. Suddenly, my career seemed so uncertain. With so many charges being brought against Michael, it was anyone's guess how things will go. Michael's improprieties and other illegal actions had put the company in jeopardy. Now we will have to wait and see where things go from here.

Chapter 12

Four Months Later

The following months after Michael's arrest, he had only admitted to overstating the company's earnings. The jury verdict was finally in on a trial that began four months earlier and capped a four-year-long government investigation on Michael. The U.S. District Court/Northern District of New York had found Michael guilty of 19 counts of conspiracy, fraud, insider trading and making false statements, which combined, carry a maximum sentence of 185 years. Luckily for Michael, he was not convicted on ten of the criminal counts. However, he was convicted of nine counts of conspiracy and fraud and will have to serve 50 years in prison for all of those counts combined. Then in a separate trial he was also found guilty on four counts of bank fraud. Michael is unlikely to get a sentence more than six months for each of those counts because he paid off the loans and the lenders suffered no economic damage.

About a week later a court official informed me that Michael's company, Manhattan Times Review, would close its doors because it was too far in the red to continue operation. This was devastating news. Now my colleagues and I were out of jobs. My heart went out to my colleagues more than for myself because many of them were not financially stable and had family responsibilities. My financial situation was great and I had no family obligations. However, I would have liked to keep the career that I loved so much.

Over the next few weeks, I stayed at home and racked my brain for some type of solution to help my colleagues and me. A promising idea came to mind, but I wasn't sure that it would work. But after thinking on the idea some more, I decided to call Chris to get his opinion.

I grabbed up the phone and dialed. The phone rang four times before Chris answered.

"Hello," his voice echoed through the phone.

"Chris — Hi — This is Rachel. How are you?"

"Well Hello Rachel! I'm wonderful — What about you? How are you holding up? I was just getting ready to call you and see if you wanted to go out to dinner this evening."

"Of course I would. A change of scenery would be great. The walls seem as though they're closing in on me. And

Chris — I would like to discuss an idea that I have with you."

"Okay. Can you be ready by five o'clock?"

"Sure."

"Alright — I'll see you at five."

Chris took me to a place called the Union Square Café on 21st street. I learned that this café served some of the most imaginative, interesting, and tasty food. I remember reading an article in Gourmet, Food & Wine about the outstanding food and superb service that people from all over savored the restaurant's marvelous dishes, their trademark hospitality, and warm décor. Now I have an opportunity to experience it firsthand.

After Chris and I were seated, we placed our order for herb-roasted chicken, fried eggplant, mashed potatoes, and sweet peas with escarole. For dessert we ordered baked banana tart with caramel and macadamia nuts. All of the food was just so delicious.

Over dessert, I brought up my idea to Chris.

"Chris — What do you think of me starting my own business or company?"

Chris seemed to be distracted a little and was looking over some files he had removed from his briefcase moments earlier.

"Are you listening to me Chris?"

"Uh - uh yes — sure. You said something about a company."

"Yes — I want to start a magazine publishing company. I believe that I can make this work and I could possibly be giving my co-workers back there jobs. I practically ran Michael's company because he was very seldom around."

"Why would you want that kind of responsibility Rachel? Anyway, you are not responsible for looking out for your co-workers. Let them take care of themselves. They're not your responsibility. Personally, I think that you would be biting off more than you can chew."

"So you don't think that I am capable of running my own company?"

"I think you are not ready for that sort of responsibility. I'm not sure you have the discipline to commit to and take on such a huge task. You are a woman for Christ's sake."

"What did you just say Chris?"

"Well — Women are not wired for being the head of a company. They are to timid to take on something like heading a company."

"So you think that women can't be leaders?"

"I just believe men make better leaders. We are hard wired for this type of stuff and we are —

"Ass holes! You're men are nothing but ass holes!" I shouted at Chris.

I abruptly stood up, grabbed my drink from the table, and dashed it in Chris's face.

"Thanks for your support," I yelled at him as I stormed out of the café.

Chris ran after me moments later and calling out my name.

"Rachel — Wait — Rachel — Wait a minute — I'm sorry — Please — Rachel."

By the time Chris had made it outside, I had slid into a cab and left him standing on the sidewalk.

When I got home I drew a hot bath of jasmine scented water and slowly eased into it. All of my muscles felt tense and I hope that the hot water would help to loosen them up. Chris had made me so furious. He didn't even try to understand what I was trying to accomplish and he didn't care. It is Chris's type of thinking that is one of the key barriers to women seeking corporate leadership.

I call Chris's beliefs gender stereotyping and it leaves women with limited, conflicting, and unfavorable options no matter how they choose to lead. It's a "damned if you do, doomed if you don't" dilemma. Chris clearly believes in the masculine leadership norm. He would not even consider the fact that I may be capable of running a company. Then there is the fact that I mostly ran Michael's company, Manhattan Times Review, because he was very seldom there. I strongly feel that I'm capable of performing a job in a CEO/President capacity.

The bath did help me to feel a little better, though a small part of me seemed to harbor some remnants of the events of my dinner with Chris. I told myself, *Rachel — don't dwell on what Chris believes. You are a very strong, independent woman. Just believe in yourself. Other women have faced this very barrier and have succeeded. You can too if you have the desire.*

After preparing for bed I slid under the silky covers. I hoped that tomorrow would bring me more contentment and that I would figure out my next action in regard to starting a company of my own.

Chapter

13

I awakened on this Sunday morning and looked over at the clock. It showed a little after seven. A small breeze stirred the curtains. The leaves of the maple tree outside the window moved slowly back and forth. I followed their rhythmic movements with my eyes as I lay half between waking and sleeping. It seemed to lull me back into a sound sleep. The next time I looked at the clock, it was eight-thirty. The ringing phone fully awakened me from my slumber, but I decided to only answer it until after the fifth ring because I presumed it was Chris calling.

"Hello," I muttered groggily.

"Rachel — It's Chris. How are you this morning?"

"How do you think Chris?" I said, drawing my eyebrows into a frown.

"Rachel — I'm sorry that I upset you last night — I mean — I wasn't trying to intentionally upset you."

"Chris — you didn't even try to understand what I was trying to talk to you about. I am capable of running my own company."

"I'm sure that you think you can, but I still say men are better suited for heading a company."

"Chris — you know what? This conversation is over. You know what else? We need some space between us for a while. I need space. So don't call me — I'll call you, okay?"

I slammed the phone on the receiver with fury. *'The nerve of him'* I thought. *How could he apologize and be critical at the same time?'*

I got out of bed, showered, dressed and made my bed. I was in the kitchen a little later making coffee. A few minutes later, the doorbell rang.

When I opened the door, there stood Romey smiling widely and looking as handsome as ever.

"Morning Romey," I said. "What are you doing here?"

Romey quickly strolled in past me and went and seated himself at the kitchen table. So I offered him coffee.

Clearing his throat, Romey looked up at me with a serious expression on his face.

"I wanted to see how you were doing since this fiasco with Michael and his company. I saw the write-up in the paper and they talked about him on the news."

I started making waffle batter as I spoke. "I've been trying to hang in there. I really don't know what to do with myself right now since I can't go into the office. But I have been working on some other projects at home."

I plugged in the waffle iron and put a pot of water on the stove with some grits in it. Romey picked up his coffee mug and walked over to lean against the counter near me. I was never good at hiding anything from Romey and I could sense he knew something was bothering me. So I quickly changed the subject to him.

"How have you and Frannie been doing? Are things better? I asked nervously.

"Rach — Frannie and I have split up. After I tried to explain to her about leaving my job and why, she got very upset with me. I told her about how unhappy I had been with my job and that my conscious bothered me so badly about how Darren and I had been obtaining property. I told her that I just couldn't do it anymore. Then she asked me what I was going to do since I had quit a really good job because I had just walked away from some damn good money. She acted like all she wanted was the money and that it didn't matter how I got it."

"Well did you tell her about your singing too?"

Yeah – I did. She really hit the ceiling then. She started ranting and raving about how stupid my singing idea was and how I could never make any money doing that. But Rach — I have been trying to talk to her for months now about how good I am at singing, but she would never listen and take me serious. She told me that she thought I was just venting and so she ignored me. Her exact words were, *"I wish you had discussed this singing business with me before you quit your job and decided to pursue it.* Anyway Rach — everything is all messed up between us now. She put me out of our bed and we haven't slept together in over a month."

"Oh Romey, I'm so sorry. I didn't know. So are you going to try to work things out with her?"

"Hell no. A week ago I had gone into Negril's Restaurant to grab a meal. While I waited for my food I happened to glance across the room. So who do I see? There's Franchesca sitting all snuggled up to some guy. They were sitting off in a cozy little corner just chatting away. So I get up and walk over to their table and surprised them both. I politely asked Frannie what was going on. She couldn't even answer me and just sat there looking stupid. So I introduced myself to the guy. As we shook hands, I asked him did he know he was with my wife. His jaw dropped momentarily and he started trying to explain about how he didn't even know she was married and that she never told him. Dude took his arm from around her, slid over and just gawked at her in disbelief. I told him that it was cool though and to enjoy their meal. I walked out of there, went home, packed my things, and went to a hotel. That's where I've been ever since."

When I looked at Romey, there was such sadness in his eyes. All I wanted was to take away the pain that he felt.

My friend didn't deserve this. Franchesca was such a fool I thought and I just kept sending him back to her to try to work things out between them. My heart went out to him and I could sense his hurt.

"I am so sorry Romey that things are so bad for you right now, I said placing my hand gently on his face.

Romey shook off his downhearted mood and returned his focus back on me. He knew that something was on my mind and I knew he was not going to let up until he found out what it was.

Now —getting back to you — you changed the subject my dear. You seem a little anxious and you look tired and not quite yourself. Tell me what's really on your mind. I want to know what's really going on with you, so spill it."

I tested the waffle iron to see if it was ready and put slices of ham in the skillet before I began to tell Romey about my conversation with Chris last night. The red light came on and the ham began to slowly sizzle in the skillet.

Romey walked over to me and took the fork from my hand and began moving the ham around in the skillet while I poured the batter for the waffles into the waffle iron.

"Rach — this reminds me of when I used to make you burnt-fried bologna sandwiches back in the day," he said smiling broadly.

"Come on Rach — talk to me."

"Romey — I tried to talk to Chris about this idea I had about starting my own company."

"And — what was his reaction to that?"

"He said that running a company is more suited for men."

Romey stopped turning the ham and abruptly turned to face me.

"He said what?"

"You know Romey, he might be right now that I think about it. There aren't any women that I know personally who head their own company," I said slowly. "Maybe I should just re-construct my ideas and —

"Stop it Rachel," Romey interrupted. "I'm not going to stand and let you feel sorry for yourself this way. You are the most intelligent woman I know. Hell you practically ran Michael's damn company on your own. Don't listen to that fool Chris. He's just hung up on his own power trip."

Romey turned the waffle iron off and the skillet. He turned to me and placed a hand on each of my shoulders and looked me straight in the eye.

"You listen to me Rachel Pendleton. If you want to start a company, I believe that you can do it. You are more than capable and you earned the respect of all your colleagues at Sunrise. You got my support — always. You can do this Rachel and please know that I'll be there if you need me for anything, alright?"

A smile slowly adorned my face. Then suddenly I threw my arms around Romey and hugged him tightly.

"Thanks Romey. You always seem to understand and support me."

"Of course Rachel — what are friends for?"

When we broke our embrace, I looked up at Romey, looking deeply into his eyes. I could see the longing in his eyes as he looked into mine. He gently kissed my forehead, then my nose. I was so caught up in the moment that I felt overcome with desire. Instinctively, I gently touched Romey's dear face and it changed and his eyes glazed over with passion. He lowered his head to bring his lips down to mine and I closed my eyes in anticipation of what was to come. Romey's tongue traced the corners of my lips and then delved inside. I basked in the feel of my hands on his chest as my tongue leisurely explored the inside of his mouth.

When Romey broke our kiss a few seconds later, it took him a few moments to get his breathing under control. The mood, the moment — everything was just right for our own personal merger. I could already imagine him warm and soft in my bed, his skin touching mine. The depth of my feelings for Romey scared me, which was the very reason why I have tried so hard to keep my distance from him. I wanted a chance to try to sort my emotions out and give me a chance to get him out of my system.

When Romey moved closer to me again, I became lost in his gaze. He began applying gentle kisses to my moist lips. After each kiss, he would intimately say how sexy I was and how horny he was. I playfully swatted his arm and he smiled that heart-melting smile of his.

Glancing up at Romey, I watched as the smile faded away and replaced by a longing, desiring gaze.

"I want to make love to you Rachel."

I opened my mouth to speak, but my voice evaded me. Then I shyly turned my head from Romey, but he gently returned it back to face him. My eyelids fluttered closed, and I felt his fingers graze my cheek with such gentleness that it caused me to slowly inhale. I felt the moist heat of his breath only seconds before he pressed his lips against my smooth forehead. I shuddered as his mouth moved and kissed my ear and cheek; then his lips traveled down my neck. Romey then brought his mouth to my lips, warm, firm, and tempting. I felt what little control I had left slip away. As the kisses became more intense, I felt as though I would float away. He slid to the corner of my lips, tasting, nibbling, then to ears, where he slowly set off little sparks within me.

Romey reclaimed my mouth again, and his fingers gripped my behind, pulling me against him, and holding me in place. I moaned as my legs gave out. Without breaking the kiss, he reached down and swept me into his arms. I knew at this point that there was no turning back and that I couldn't stop what was happening even if I wanted to.

With me still in his arms, he was headed for the bedroom when the couch beckoned him. Romey decided that the couch was closer and changed his course.

He deposited me on the cushions, and then lay down with the weight of his body resting between my legs. He covered my mouth again hungrily. His lips trailed from my lips marking a path of wet kisses as he slipped one hand beneath my blouse. My breath caught when his fingers touched my warm, soft skin. His fingers feathered over the slope of my body just barely brushing one gloriously firm breast. I made a noise deep in my throat that sounded just like a purr. The need between my legs was rising and becoming stronger and stronger. I arched my body into his hand.

Heat rushed through me, setting low in my body. "Romey," I groaned, breaking our kiss. "What are you trying to do —," I whispered as my words were swallowed up by Romey's lips.

When Romey broke the kiss and leaned back slightly, I stared up at him, waiting and wondering, stunned at my own emotions.

Romey gently removed my clothing and quickly removed his own except his boxers, and then resumed his position next to me.

"You are so beautiful," he whispered, mesmerized, his eyes glazed with passion.

Romey watched me as a wicked smile spread across my features. I thought to myself, *Man, what would it feel like to wake up every morning to a smile that made so many sinful promises?*

I wriggled my way around on the couch until Romey was the one lying on his back: then I leaned over him. He bit back a groan as my fingernails grazed his abdomen and sending ripples of excitement through his body. He obliged me by lifting his hips so that I could slide his boxers from his body. When I stood before him, his eyes drank in the vision of my swollen breasts.

My heart pounded furiously as I stood there, my body responding to his gaze, silently struggling, begging to be touched. Then Romey did touch me, reaching out for me, his warm hands cupping my swollen breasts. His hands kneaded my breasts, and his thumbs made devastatingly arousing circles over each chocolate nipple, drawing them into hard, pebbled peaks. I trembled, unable to hold back my excitement as his hand stroked my moist sensitive area. All at once, I hoped the moment would go on, hoped it would end, hoped I could survive the intense pleasure, which I knew was still coming.

With a muffled oath, he pulled me back down on top of him. Our bodies came together, warm, naked, trembling, skin against skin, and I felt an indescribable desire pour over me in turbulent waves. The tips of my breasts tingled where they touched the coarse, curly hair on his chest, and when he moved his hand down my back, a trail of fire blazed in its wake.

I felt Romey's hands slide down and cup my bottom. His hands were strong as he grasped me, pulling me closer. Our lips met in a frantic search for closeness. His tongue traveled deeper, tangling with mine, drawing out hot, feverish cries. His hands began to spread liquid fire over my skin, down my hips and thighs. His fingers brushed through the soft mound of hair, seeking the hidden nub of pleasure within, and found mine, wet and ready. I gasped, my need for him slipping out in moans against his mouth.

"Romey," I whispered as he rolled me beneath him. "That feels so good."

Lowering his head, he dropped soft kisses on tips of my breasts. He drew one sensitive bud into his mouth. The sensation of his tongue, hot and wet, caressing my beaded nipple caused me to sigh with pleasure.

At this point, Romey was driving me mad; bringing forward feelings I didn't know existed. I was grateful that he was taking his time so that I had a chance to experience each and every pleasurable moment.

Drifting lower, Romey's lips left a heated path as he kissed under my breasts and down along the line of my stomach. His tongue lapped at my navel, drawing a circle around the indentation, then indulging at the deep center, sending delicious shudders down the length of me and making me whimper.

"Rachel — you're a beautiful and sexy woman," Romey said, his voice husky.

I released a sound of sheer frustration. "Romey, please —," I muttered as his lips closed over an aching nipple. "I need —," The rest of my words were lost to a loud gasp.

Romey shifted his weight and moved between my wobbly legs, caressing my inner thighs. Then with his hand, he drew a straight line right down to my source of desire. He touched the bud and felt me tense with pleasure.

"What?" his voice was a low, thrilling whisper as he slipped one finger into my heated core. "Baby, tell me what you need."

"To feel you," I moaned, pushing my hips up against his hands. "Please Romey I —"

He inserted another finger then flicked and swirled as he increased the rhythm, drawing agonizing cries from my lungs. I dug my fingernails into his arms, my hips rising to meet each thrust. "Please, Romey. I need you now." I moaned.

He kissed me once more, and then rose. I released a frustrated cry at his abrupt departure. He had disappeared in the other room for what seemed like hours, when it was just a few excruciating moments. As I lay on the couch, I saw the light flip on in the bedroom. I smiled when he returned. He had sheathed himself. Returning to the couch, he pulled me back into his arms and positioned himself above me.

Something inside me wound up like a watch spring as he kissed me deeply. I wrapped my legs around his hips and felt him pulsing at the opening of my desire. Slanting his hips, he gently penetrated me, inch by glorious inch. Everything tensed in my body, and I moaned. Romey was larger than I'd expected him to be, filling me completely. He paused, giving me time to adjust; then I raised my hips to meet his thrusts, drawing him deeper inside me. He murmured my name against my cheek as he began to move inside me, slowly, and smoothly, until together we found the sweet, deep rhythm of pleasure. My breathing came in erotic gasps as we flew higher and higher to the heights of passion. I sank into the couch, holding on as I met every move. My resolve was shattered. My body began to vibrate, my legs trembled, my last strand of control slipped further, far beyond my reach. I moved my body with his, encouraging him to take me fully. He reached under and clenched my buttocks, angling my hips for deeper entry, and thrust strongly into me until I shattered into a million tiny fragments, holding on to him, crying out his name as a climax took over. Romey released a deep grunt, spilling into with a spasm of ecstasy.

As his breathing resumed, he rolled off me and fell onto the floor. Hearing my light giggles, he reached up and gently pulled me down on top of him. My laughter continued, but I didn't resist when he scooped me up into his arms and carried me to bed. He joined me under the covers and held me until we both had fallen into a deep, satisfied slumber.

Chapter

14

Well past lunchtime, I woke up to sunlight skimming through the curtains and the sound of Romey humming off key in the shower.

Closing my eyes again, I tried to persuade myself that what had happened between Romey and me hadn't happened. *How could I have been so weak I thought? I had slept with my best friend who by the way is still married.*

Shame washed over me like a tidal wave as conflicting emotions raged through my mind. I loved Romey but this had been all wrong.

I abruptly jumped out of bed and put on my robe, trying to get a handle on my thoughts and feelings.

Romey suddenly stepped out of the bathroom clad only in a towel.

"Well hello beautiful. You're awake," he said smiling broadly.

"Yea – yea – I - I'm awake, I managed to stutter out.

Romey could see that I had something on my mind and came over closer to me, looking very concerned.

"What's wrong? What's that look Rach?"

"Look — uh – uh – Romey. What just happened between us was a mistake. It shouldn't have happened and it can never happen again."

"But Rach I —

"It can't happen again Romey. You are a married man and I'm practically engaged," I spouted with attitude.

"You 're not going to tell —

"No — I'm not going to tell Chris, but you need to get dressed and go."

"But Rachel, why are you so —

I shot Romey an evil glare. "Just go — now, okay?"

"Okay, okay. I'm going."

Romey quickly dressed and left, but not without giving me that sadden, "I don't understand what just happened" look.

After Romey left, I showered and plopped down on the couch, trying to analyze what he and I had done. Guilt was consuming me and I felt like a traitor to both Frannie and Chris. *Why couldn't I have maintained my control with Romey? I had done so well for years. My resistance wore down for a moment and I succumbed and gave in to my emotions. As much as I love Romey, I cannot allow my emotions to take control again. You really have messed up girl I scolded myself.*

I'll just have to put distance between Romey and me. Maybe that will help I thought."

I had to get the thoughts of Romey off my mind. There was an article I had started some months back that I'd been doing background on. Working on it will get my mind on something constructive instead of the huge mess I've made of my life. I'll just throw myself into my work. That should help me to get perspective on my life again.

Over the next few weeks, I worked on my article. It was about Motown history. I had started work on this article some time ago, but had placed it on the backburner. My article would be great writing and I could possibly get high recognition for publishing it. What better person to do a history on Motown than the Motown girl herself who has loved that music since I was a kid.

The Motown sound has helped shape soul music history and it was "the sound" when I was growing up and I still love it. I was doing an in-depth write up of several groups in the 70's that contributed to Motown's music history.

One group that I was fond of was Philadelphia's most famous Soul Empire — Kenny Gamble and Leon Huff's Philadelphia International Records, home of the O'Jays, The Intruders, Harold Melvin & the Blue Notes, the Three Degrees, and Billy Paul. And there were the heavyweights like the Stylistics and the Delfonics that made Thom Bell/

Linda Creed School of Philly Soul huge. The Blue Magic hit big in 1974, with their smooth, polished sound with the help of the Bell/Creed School.

There was one LP that demonstrated that Blue Magic was a fine group in their own right. The single that put Blue Magic on the map was *Sideshow*, a hit ballad that was as clever as it was melancholy. *Sideshow* described a circus, but not an ordinary circus — a circus in which all of the attractions were noteworthy because of their terrible luck when it came to romantic relationships. The tune was brilliant; like so many great blues and country gems. *Sideshow* finds a witty way to talk about romantic disappointments.

I really could relate to the song *Sideshow* because of my failed relationships and especially my failure to acknowledge my true feelings for Roman Sinclair. I now felt like one of those sideshow attractions Blue Magic's song *Sideshow*. I haven't managed to stay in any of my relationships for more than a few months so I definitely would fit into this lovelorn circus. I am just a friend to Romey and feel that this is the way it will always be and that's all I've ever been to him. I'm just a girl who wants to be the center of his world and I only have my heart and soul to offer. I fear that my love wouldn't be enough for him to notice me as his woman and not just his friend. I tried so hard to smile when he's with another and try to act like everything is ok when I know deep down that it's not. I know now how it feels to be so in love with someone who doesn't even know it. Romey invades my dreams and I see us both together constantly, he's just not able to see this love that's there inside me. It hurts to see him look at Frannie with love in his eyes and with me it's only a friendship. I wonder what does he see in her that he can't see in me and that he shows her love but there is none for me. I guess Romey is and always will be my secret love.

Chapter 15

I arose early this morning and put the finishing touches on my story. After pouring a cup of coffee, I stepped out on my small terrace and took in the wondrous breeze that was stirring outside. The distant city sounds was softened by the lap of water against the waterfront pilings. As I stood in the midst of my tranquil surroundings, my mind wondered to a place of uncertainty. Slight tension flowed through every channel of my being and I felt somewhat keyed up — but yet — in limbo. Romey's strong belief in me heading my company had inspired soul-searching. Compelling my innermost self with courage and fortitude, I brought every thought, every emotion, and every intention to the light. And after carefully emomuating all of my thoughts, I could envision all of the possibilities before me. I thought, why did I allow Chris to dissuade me from my dreams and goals? I can do this — I know I can. My goal was to run my own company and I'm going to follow through with it.

Over the next few weeks, I began working toward my goal of attaining my own business. After assuring that Manhattan Times Review was indeed for sale, I had to go about the tedious task of acquiring the needed finances to purchase the building. Knowing that I had to convince some serious people that I really need the money, I wanted to be savvy enough to excite them into lending me the money that I need. Convincing them to part with the money would be the most important *"sale"* I could ever make, so I wanted to get it right.

Near the end of the second week, my loan proposal had come together and I was now ready and armed with a reliable proposal that I would be able to face the loan officer with confidence. I phoned and made an appointment to speak with a loan officer at Newtek Small Business Finance Inc., which was one of several small business lenders in New York. The loan officer had introduced himself as Kyle Martin and asked me to come in on Friday morning at ten a.m. to discuss my proposal. He gave me the location of the office complex and added that he was on the third floor of that building.

Today was the big day that could possibly decide my future at attaining my dream of becoming an entrepreneur — but I was ready. I arrived at the office at a quarter to ten and made my way upstairs to the third floor office suites.

I searched the wall-mounted directory until I found Kyle Martin's name. When I reached his office, his secretary alerted him of my arrimom and then she directed me to his office.

After a few hours, the meeting with Kyle was over. We had discussed everything that involved the loan process and he commended me on how detailed my proposal had been and was impressed with my 5 C's of credit: capacity, capital, collateral, condition, and character. Also, Kyle added that for the particular building that I wanted to purchase the price had been reduced dramatically to make sure it could be sold. He said that they weren't sure they would get an interested buyer in light of some of the negative publicity the company had gotten during Michael's tenure. Kyle told me that I should hear from him within forty-eight hours.

The time that I waited for Kyle's phone call seemed to almost stand still. My anticipation had started to grow and I 'd hoped that the impression I had made on Kyle was as good as he'd said. Busing myself with mundane chores helped to past the time, but the waiting still tugged at my mind from time to time.

Walking to the closet, I removed fresh bed linen from the overhead shelf and changed my bed. After fluffing my pillows, I grabbed one up and caressed it to my chest. The fresh, clean scent of the silky pillowcase was delightful to my senses. I lay across the bed still clinging to the pillow as my mind wondered off to thoughts of how great my company could be if this loan went through for me.

Around two-thirty in the afternoon on the third day, the phone rang. I was a little scared and anxious at the same time, but I answered the phone confidently.

"Ms. Pendleton? This is Kyle Martin at Newtek Small Business Finance."

"Hello Mr. Martin — how are you?"

"I'm doing great thank you and how are you?"

"I'm doing okay, I'm just feeling a bit anxious."

"There's no need to feel anxious Ms. Pendleton. I have some wonderful news for you. Your loan was approved and it didn't even take the entire four days to process."

Doing a little jig with my hand covering the speaking end of the receiver, I said softly, "Yes – yes – yes." "Thank you so much Mr. Martin."

"Great then. Now if you can come in the morning, we can finalize the paperwork and get you your money."

"I will be there bright and early."

"Wonderful. I'll see you then, okay? Goodbye."

I was on cloud nine because I could now start my business. Naming my business would be the next task. I decided on the name Dalána Publishing. Dalana was my middle name and I like how it sounded with the word Publishing behind it. I thought that it had a nice enough ring to it.

After naming my company, I still had a few things left to do. I felt certain that my business would be profitable so I concentrated on other details such as getting permits, insurance, and hiring a staff. The equipment was still there from when Michael had the building, so I didn't need to purchase more at this time.

As for the staff, an idea came to me. I wondered if my former colleagues would be interested in working under my leadership. After making some calls, I found that all of Michael's former staff wanted to work for me. They were all very good, dependable people, which I'd learned from being under Michael's administration.

My company was to be a sole proprietorship. I was now an entrepreneur and had many fresh ideas for my company. Though Michael had messed up his life, he had always inspired and supported me when I was his editor. Now, I was ready to jump into my new business with both feet. My longtime dream had finally come true.

Chapter

16

Two Years Later

My magazine company had been flourishing over the past year. At this rate, my magazine will turn a hefty profit before my working capital is exhausted. The company is already making a profit and my loan officer is very happy with how well my business is doing. My staff has done an excellent job meeting all dealines. Everyone seems happy and pleased with my administration. Business life was great, but my social life was practically non-existant. It was Friday and time to go home and I had no plans for the weekend. Over the past years all I had been doing was concentrating on my business and working on various personal writing articles. All business and no play has made me a very dull and boring individual. Yet, I still found time to reflect on Romey and my own personal life. I had dreamed of my own wedding one day for most of my life, yet I still remain single and for the most part, dateless. Can you say loser?

Of course, if I hadn't secretly given my heart to my best friend, who'd I'd sworn off ever getting physically involved with, I might not be in this predicament. Opportunities for long lasting love had always seemed to somehow evade me, due to my tunnel vision on the subject and the fact that many of the men I had dated could never seem to get their shit together. At twelve years of age I'd decided that Roman Sinclair was *the one*. And that childish certainly had rooted deeply within me and only flourished with time.

For the last few years she'd done her best to stay away from him. I had placed the bulk of my concentration and time on running my company with a small percentage dealing with the " on again/off again" relationship Chris and I had. Romey and I still occasionally talked on the phone, but I still advised myself to not be in close proximity of him. Being in his sphere filled my heart with an unbearable ache. I felt that my dreams were hopeless. As a married, successful, and let's not forget good-looking guy, he had Franchesca in his life and I wanted to respect that even though I felt that she didn't really appreciate nor truly love Romey. There were times that I had wished that I could surgically remove him from her heart. All Franchesca seemed to want was money, money, and more money. She absolutely refused to support him on anything. She really needed to be exorcised right out of his life. But I had no say so in that matter — that decision would have to be totally up to Romey. And this weekend looks like another weekend of TV dinners, Chinese Take-out, and romance novels.

After getting home, I had taken a nice long bath and put on my loungewear and robe. Then I poured a glass of chardonnay, grabbed my book, and plopped on the sofa to get comfortable. Three chapters into my book, my quiet moment was broken by the ringing doorbell.

To my surprise, it was Chris. I hadn't seen him in quite some time so it was a little unexpected to see him standing at my door.

"Hello Rachel —I know that I should have called first before coming over, but I was afriad you would invent some sort of excuse not to see me. May I come in?"

"I probably should close the door in your face, but my heart won't hold on to grudges," I said with a serious glint in my eye.

Opening the door wider, I motioned for him to come on inside.

"So — how have you been lately Rachel?"

"I'm good. My business is doing very well and I'm busy a lot attending to publishing details and running my company. I hardly have time for anthing else," I said with a sheepish half-smile.

"Well you're not so busy right now are you?"

"I'm just chillin, catching up on some reading and —-

"Go for a leisurely stroll with me," Chris interrupted. "Just go and get dressed and go for a walk with me okay? Please? It's so nice out tonight. And you can even dress casual if you want. See — I'm not in a suit and tie."

"I – I – don't know Chris. I don't think I —

"It'll be fun I promise. You will enjoy yourself."

Looking at Chris and hearing him plead with me to go with him felt good. I felt that it served him right for listening to his sarcastic remarks over the years toward my capabilities of running my own company. Now he's standing here with a "goofy as hell" smile pleading with me to go out with him.

"Oh all right Chris. Let me go and change and I'll be right out."

Disappearing into my bedroom, I changed into a pair of jeans and a fresh cotton shirt, which I knotted at the waist, slipped on a pair of navy tennis shoes, brushed my hair, and brushed on a dab of burgundy blusher before rejoining Chris in the living room.

"You look great Rachel. Come on — let's go. It's nearly dark and I can guarantee that the place I have in mind for us to walk to is small and definitely off the beaten path. So you don't really have to worry about appearances so much. We can just relax and enjoy the evening, okay?" Chris said walking toward the kitchen.

"Okay Chris — but I don't want to be out very late."

"I promise not to keep you out late if you promise to give me some answers about us.

From his firm stance in the kitchen archway, Chris undauntedly held my gaze. He had a glint in his eye that made me feel he was up to something.

"Come on," he coaxed, cocking his head in such a innocent way that the harshness vanished from my face.

Sighing heavily in capitulation, I relaxed.

"I'm a fool is what I am for letting you talk me into this. You must feel very proud of yourself."

I had expected him to enjoy the moment's opportunity for gloating at his success in getting me to go out with him. But contrary to my expectations, Chris grew pensive.

"Proud?" he asked, as if not comprehending. "No — not proud."

When he frowned, he looked every bit of his thirty-four years."I'd simply like — your company."

Since Chris had put it that way, I couldn't refuse him. *Loneliness.* That was what struck me. Indeed we did have that in common.

As he had pointed out, it was nearly dark when we emerged from my apartment and started up the hill. There were other walkers along the route, some of whom I recognized as neighbors. But I felt comfortable. After his exchange of suit and tie for denim and its more casual accoutrements, Chris looked really nice. Looking up at him as we made our leisurely climb, I wondered who was this man — really.

"Okay," he began with good-natured irony. "I'm listening?"

"Listening?" I playfully spouted back.

"Uh – huh. You said you'd give me some answers. It's time to settle up."

I just shook my head and looked nonchalant.

"Not until we've got dinner in front of us. If I tell you now, you're apt to turn around and go back."

"Oh no, I wouldn't do that. I want your company for longer than that Rachel."

So I did talk to Chris about us, but I couldn't be quite as blunt. It was dark, yes, and indeed romantic now, but all in a very gentle, kind of way.

There were other things about Chris that bothered me. I had always tried to support him in his endeavors and had gone to nearly all of his social engagements, said all of the right things to his VIP's and laughed at all of their jokes. They loved me and had told Chris that I was definitely a keeper. But Chris never seemed to be able to support me in none of my affairs or believed in what I was doing. Chris had wanted us to get I know, but I had not been certain that I should since he couldn't be there for me as I had been for him.

Chris took my hand to pull me back from the curb while a car charged up one side of Joy Street and down the other. My hand remained clasped in his when we slowly started across the street ourselves. He squeezed my hand and led me on. As we passed beneath the State House Arch, its light illuminated both our faces. For an instant, we stopped, and then continued on our journey.

The golden dome of the State House was behind us now as we made our way down the opposite side of the hill toward City Hall Plaza and the marketplace beyond. The strength of Chris's hand in mine so very gently attested to the world of other treasures embodied in this man.

We walked in silence for a while then, enjoying the Saturday night life of the city with its summertime enchantment. We passed open-air restaurants and brightly lit shops. They meandered among people similarly meandering, people of all ages, tourist and native alike. Amid the crowd we were anonymous, our faces dimly lit by the gaslights cordoning the walks of the harbor.

It was as though the shades of night had blunted our differences, as though we were a pair, a unit weaving among others. Chris guided me gently, his arm lightly around my back now to ease me beside him toward our destination. When we reached it, a small private seafood house, I felt delightfully mellow.

"So — did I come through for you?" Chris asked, bending down to murmur in my ear as he held the chair out for me in a courtly manner.

"You did come through for me Chris," I smiled, giving credit where credit is due. "This really is off the beaten path. Actually this place was down several alleys and a harbor side path."

Chris settled into a seat opposite of mine.

"That's why this place is so pleasant. It mainly serves residents of the harbor area itself."

"Not bad," I said admirably looking over the place. "Not bad at all. It's a nice place and right in the heart of the city. I like it. And you eat here how often?

"Maybe once a week or so. They have got a lot of great stuff in here. Why don't you look at the menu and decide what you want."

Leaving the menu untouched and in its place, I tilted my head sideways. "I've got a better idea. You order. Surprise me."

It seemed like a fun idea I thought and very different from my usual style.

"Are you game Chris?"

Chris's mouth twitched in the start of a daring smile.

"I'm game," he matched it.

Staring at me a moment longer, he seemed to weigh and balance the extent of my adventurousness. Then, without further word, he motioned to the waitress. Within minutes, a bottle of wine had been uncorked and two glasses filled and raised in a toast.

Only then did Chris hesitate. I waited expectantly, wondering what sort of eloquence I'd hear. He seemed about to start more than once before catching his breath and beginning again.

"Cheers !" he said at last, and I grimaced.

"Cheers? That's profound," I said giggling.

"What — you've got something better?" he asked amused.

"Sure," I replied boldly. "If I wanted to. But right now, I'd like to ask you a few questions."

"Go ahead — I'll give you an answer if I can."

"Have you read any of my articles or writing?"

Chris shrugged, and then frowned as though trying to come up with an acceptable answer for me.

"Some. I think your writing is great Rachel. You know that," He said with uncertainty.

"Care to elaborate on them. Better yet, just tell me about any one of them — your choice," I said, searching his face for any clue that he may have actually read an article of mine.

When Chris dipped his head in silent admission, I realized that he hadn't read any of my work at all.

Chris moved his wine glass to make room for the salad that he chose at that moment to appear at their places. I studied the creation before me and nodded in agreement.

"This is quite a salad. There must be three kinds of lettuce here, not to mention zucchini, chickpeas and bean sprouts. With the help of a fork, I peered beneath a carrot curl.

Chris popped a cherry tomato into his mouth and slightly smiled at my momentary satisfaction and pleasure.

"You've forgotten to mention cucumbers, tomatoes, and Spanish onions," he said.

"Oh no," I came back as I nonchalantly sucked the pit out of an over-sized black olive. "You're not getting off that easily. But I will table the question I asked you for now until we finish our meal."

Two hours later, as we slowly retraced our steps from the waterfront through Government Center, up over the hill and down again to my place, we were still in agreement. The meal we'd shared had been delicious — every last shrimp, scallop, and oyster that Chris had ordered.

"I feel absolutely stuffed." I let out a forced breath. "I only wish I had the strength to jog up and down the hill a few times," I remarked.

When Chris and I reached my place, he stopped still before it.

"I've really enjoyed your company tonight Rachel. Maybe we can do this again soon?"

I lowered my head to grope in my purse for my keys. When I looked up again, I admired the full arch of Chris's brow and how it had scattered furrows in its wake.

"Look – Chris. It's hard for me to accept the fact that you don't try to be involved in any of my interests. I would have thought that you would have read some of my work. That really hurts — especially in light that I had always been there for you — supporting and encouraging — believing and offering you my undivided attention on all of your pursuits and dreams. As much as I enjoyed spending time with you tonight, I just can't pursue a personal relationship with you at this time. I'm sorry — I really am Chris."

Chris now looked distraught and I knew it was because of what I had just said. But I needed to be honest with him and myself. I know that I wanted someone who would be there for me in every way. I didn't feel that Chris was capable of a deep love and emotional commitment like that. Chris forced a half smile as he struggled to accept the decision I had made.

"So — this is it Rachel. We are really and truly breaking up for good."

Chris locked eyes with me and I kept my gaze inscrutable.

"I'm sorry Chris," I replied honestly. "I just think that this is for the best."

Chris lowered his head, and then raised it just a bit to look at me through spiky, brown lashes. Slowly and with devastating implication, he shook his head.

"What do you mean — you're sorry?" he asked with such sharpness that my stomach knotted. "You know — this is some cold shit. But that's okay. I can find someone else. Who the hell needs you anyway? And don't worry Rachel — I won't be calling you and I won't be back."

"Chris — don't be so —

"Don't be so what — angry? Well, I am angry, but I'll forget about you."

Chris spun around on his heel to leave, and then he stopped abruptly. Turning back to face me, he allowed his eyes to express his boiling rage momentarily. I stared incomprehensibility at this entity who had invaded the Chris I thought I knew.

"By the way — you will fail miserably at running your company. I told you — women aren't capable of such a task as heading a company," he blurted angrily. "Good luck to you — you will need it."

Chris stormed off, leaving me standing there in shock from his last comments. Struggling to regroup, I let myself into my apartment and locked the door behind me. Still fully dressed, I lay across my bed in dismay. It wasn't until the wee hours of the morning that I was able to accept what had happened between Chris and me.

I had anguished late and woke up early, determined to read through the the Sunday paper. Yet my mind wandered to thoughts of Chris. So I decided to shower, put on a pair of denim shorts and a tee, and pour myself a cup of coffee. Aimless steps took me out on the balcony. The warm breeze ruffled my hair as I stood at the railing admiring the city before me. With a sigh of resignation, I settled into the chaise lounge chair out there. I thought to myself, this is no day for the Sunday paper. What I wanted was *endless enchantment.* But first I feel that I really need to get away for a while. The change of scenery would probably do me good. It would give me a chance to regroup. Without a care for the why of it all, I reached for my book and opened chapter one. I was right back at the start.

Chapter 17

Morning found me in the kitchen making coffee before my alarm clock went off. I decided to go to the fitness center this morning to work out before going to work. My muscles were stiffened from all of the tension and stress that Chris had helped to create.

After my workout, I returned to my apartment for a quick shower and a cup of coffee before heading for the office. It was seven-thirty A.M. when I arrived at the office and Tina and the rest of the crew were already there. Tina had been my secretary under Michael's administration, but since she had shown so much interest in editing of the magazine, I had decided on grooming her to be an editor. Tina was overjoyed at the idea of one day becoming an editor here.

Tina had given me my messages that had come through before my arrival at the office this morning and returned to her desk. I looked over the messages and found one to be interesting from a Reginald Anderson. Peeked from curiosity, I phoned him to see what his message meant. After speaking with Mr. Anderson, I learned that he had been a former contact of Michael. He had learned of my excellent work through Michael and wanted to ask if I would do a project for him. The project was to oversee publicity for a rich African-American group that is opening a guest ranch, spa and resort in Tucson, Arizona. Mr. Anderson had offered me a generous payment for this project and would also pay my expenses for taking the trip to complete the assignment. He also told me that he would like to come into the office and discuss the details. I agreed and hung up the phone.

My mind reflected on the conversation that I had with Mr. Anderson. The assignment was out West and that was another area of the world I had not had the pleasure to travel. This may be just what I need — get away for a while I thought. I realize that this is work, but I'm sure that I won't be working all of the time. I decided to do some research on the city where I would go to on the assignment — Tucson, Arizona.

I found out that this was really a wonderful place. *If you can daydream it, you could definitely do it here.* Tucson is the kind of town you daydream about - there are endless ways to relax, rejuvenate and reinvigorate. Tucson is a relaxed, friendly and welcoming community. Though the metro-area population is just over one million residents, the city is as comfortable as a small town. Tucsonans seem to pride themselves in their progressiveness and social consciousness. It's a genuinely inclusive community where all are welcome and diversity is embraced. The people there are said to be friendly and down to earth, the scenery is awe-inspiring, and the variety of world-class attractions and things to do is unparalleled. It is said to be the experience of a lifetime, classy, delicious and warmly welcoming, has unsurpassed beauty …casual and relaxing, yet elegant. Why in the world would anyone stay anywhere else?

Whether you are parents of prospective students, or visiting your current students, celebrating a graduation or are on official college business, the Royal Elizabeth is also an ideal place to stay for your visit to the *University of Arizona.* We are one mile from the Main Gate of the historic campus which makes for a pleasant walk or bike ride in moderate temperatures or a very short drive otherwise. On Friday evenings and all day Saturdays and Sundays you may also ride the historic *Old Pueblo Trolley* to the *University's Main Gate.* The trolley terminus is a short six block walk from The Liz, and, by late 2009 the Old Pueblo Trolley is expected to share a part of its route with a new *light rail line* to better connect Tucson's Westside and Downtown to the University and the *University Medical Center* campus. In addition to the electric streetcar division, OPT has a number of historic buses, and the recently opened *Southern Arizona Transportation Museum* at the downtown Historic Depot.

In a prime location near downtown Tucson and just outside Tucson International Airport, the Award winning Country Inn Tucson Hotel provides the kind of cozy accommodations, friendly services and warm touches that make this Tucson hotel a great choice for business or pleasure.

Arizona is a popular location for filming, whether it's a full-length feature, a TV commercial or a print ad. The state's Film Office provides an array of services for filming at city-owned sites and other locations throughout the metropolitan areas. Among the services provided are initial location scouting, productions and film permit information and acting as a liaison between your company, government offices and the community. You'll also find practical information and a photo gallery of potential film locations, including airports, homes, mountains and deserts, parks, rivers, farms and churches.

Arizona is a very beautiful place filled with great people. Beautiful vistas, spectacular mountains, bustling modern cities or old, turn-of-the-century small towns can be found in this diverse state. Great locations, experienced crews, and all the equipment you need under the bright sun -- this is a great place to shoot!

Arizona has enjoyed a long history of hosting productions. Starting with the first western in Tucson in the early 1920s to the multi-camera reality show shot recently in Maricopa, the state of Arizona has welcomed all. So whether a big or small feature film, a national commercial, a television series or a knockout multi-media program at a world-class resort, producers have found the talent, the crew and the gear here in Arizona necessary to meet their goals for success.

Arizona is the home of Phoenix, Tucson, Lake Mead, Grand Canyon National Park, Flagstaff, Lake Havasu City, Navajo Indian Reservation, Lake Powell, Yuma, Nogales, Scottsdale, Petrified Forest, and Tombstone.

There were some popular movies filmed in Tucson: Alice Doesn't Live Here Anymore (1974), Arizona (1940), Bodies, Rest and Motion (1993), Boys on the Side (1995), C.C. and Company (1970), Can't Buy Me Love (1987), Dance with the Devil (1997), Flashpoint (1984), Harley Davidson and the Marlboro Man (1991), Hombre (1967), How the West Was Won (1962), Jesus' Son (1999), A Kiss Before Dying (1956), Lilies of the Field (1963), Major League (1989), The Postman (1997), Revenge of the Nerds (1984), Revenge of the Nerds II: Nerds in Paradise (1987), Rio Bravo (1959), A Star Is Born (1976), Stir Crazy (1980), Terminal Velocity (19946), The Three Amigos (1986), Thunder Alley (1985), Tin Cup (1996), and Tombstone (1993).

Tucson also has the wonderful *Royal Elizabeth Bed & Breakfast Inn* that is a true historic landmark. A significant part of the Royal Elizabeth experience—and what makes this experience unique over all others—is living within the magnificent surroundings of one of Arizona's oldest homes.

The assignment kind of excited me and I found myself anxious for Mr. Anderson's arrimom. Putting my mind on other duties, looked briefly at my other messages Tina had given me and decided which ones needed my immediate attention. I sent off some urgent emails to a few clients. I ended each email with *If there is anything else I can help you with, please contact my office.* I took pride in making myself available to my clients and liked being able to service their needs as quickly as possible.

Suddenly, Tina buzzed my phone, "Rachel, Reginald Anderson is here to see you."

"Thank you Tina — you may send him in," I replied.

"Good morning Rachel," he greeted.

"Hello, Reginald," I said, as I looked him in the eyes.

I noticed that another of Michael's associates was with Reginald. "Gary, I didn't know that you were going to be joining us, I said as I eyed Reginald suspiciously. "This must be a big one for you to come in this early."

Gary gave me a polite kiss on the cheek as he pulled my chair out for me. "Rachel, this is big. That's why I want to make sure you're on board for this project."

The two men sat, and Gary explained the details of the project. "Rachel, we have on our hands a group of very wealthy African-Americans who are friends of my wife. I'm sure Reginald has told you that this group is opening a ranch and spa in Tucson, Arizona. The grand opening is in one month. They just don't feel like they are getting the kind of exposure they need for the kind of clientele they want to attract."

He handed me a brochure of the resort and I looked at the cover. I saw the beautiful building that obviously was the resort. In the forefront of the picture stood three very tall, incredibly handsome African-American cowboys. I opened the brochure and began reading its contents.

I brought my attention back to the meeting. "I understand all that, Gary. What I don't understand is why it is so important that I take this client. Reginald said that you, as well as the client, wanted only me. Why?" I asked, already knowing that I would accept the assignment just to have a chance to leave Manhattan for a while.

Reginald and Gary smiled at each other before Gary said, "Rachel, that would be your personal cheerleader's fault."

"Angela," I said, knowing just whom he was talking about. Angela was Gary's wife, and everyone in the office teased me about how the wife of one of Michaels's VIP associates was my number-one fan. Even Gary teased me about it. Angela had been immensely impressed with me ever since I pulled her butt out of the fire several years back on the Hastings account.

Philip and Marcia Hastings of Hastings Fiber Optics had needed a public relations representative. Angela had offered to find them someone at the Manhattan Times Review and had selected Randy Osborne at random, who Michael eventually fired later. Randy bombed on the account, and Angela was desperate to save face with the Hastings. I was new, and the only editor available, so Gary asked me to take on the mess. I handled the account like a seasoned veteran, and Angela had been singing my praises ever since.

I should have known it had something to do with Angela." I smiled as I shook my head.

"Rachel, this account is huge. Even if Angela hadn't insisted on you handling the account, I would have. You're smooth, smart, and very efficient. You're just the person for the job. So, are you on board?" Gary asked me directly.

"You already know I'm on board, Gary. I'd do anything for my favorite cheerleader," I said with a wink.

Gary winked back. "Thanks Rachel," he said as he stood to leave. Reginald will fill you in on all of the particulars."

"Tell Angela that I said hello and give her my love," I told him as he begun to leave.

"I sure will," he replied. "Now, if you'll excuse me, I have to get back to my own office. There are a few things that I have to do before I meet Donozo and Jeffries for golf at the Sierra La Verne Country Club."

"Sierra La Verne Country Club? Isn't that in Southern California?" I asked him, a confused look on my face.

"That would be true, Rachel, Thank goodness Donozo has a company jet at his disposal, huh?" He laughed as he left the room.

"What a character," I said to Reginald.

"Yeah, I wish my friends had a company jet they could use any time they wanted," Reginald said with a smirk on his face.

"I have friends who would be quite happy with that Hummer and thirty-five-foot boat you have. You shouldn't complain."

"Who's' complaining?" he joked. Turning serious, he said, "Well, Rachel, you'll be leaving Sunday night. Cates, Chaney, and Simpson, the primary investors who have hired us, won't be at the ranch until the grand opening."

"Who is my contact person there?" I asked.

"Teresa Simpson is the manager. She has already faxed us everything we need. Eric, from LTI (Lifestyle Transportation International) Limousine Service, will be picking you up to take you to the airport. You get into Tucson at two P.M., and Teresa says that she will be waiting for you."

"What's my expense account looking like?"

"The sky is the limit. The investors want you to have everything you need to make this opening magnificent," he said, handing me an envelope and Teresa's business card.

I opened the envelope and removed its contents. It was an American Express business card, with a note that read If you need anything else, let Teresa know, she will be sure to get it for you. Thanks, Nathaniel Cates. I looked up with a slight smile on my face; I bounced my eyebrows. Reginald bounced his back.

"I'll have Helen arrange your flight and then I'll get back with you."

"Reginald, I think I want to start out earlier than Sunday. I'm going home for a few days."

"Chicago?"

"Yes. I'm going to visit my family. I want to leave early Thursday. Will that be okay?"

"Absolutely not, I'll have Helen take care of that for you."

"Thanks Reginald," I said as I followed him to the door. "You know, I'm kind of excited about this trip. I think I need to get away for a while. How long do you think I'll be out there?"

"Hmmm, I'm thinking you'll only need to be there for a week or two. But you'll have to go back again for the opening. Then again, you can stay the whole month if you want, just play it by ear."

"Sounds good to me, Reginald, thanks," I said waving good-bye.

I quickly walked back to my desk, pleased with my assignment. I had mountains of work to finish and tons of things to do before Thursday. I knew that I could rely on Tina to take care of the office work while I'm away, but I had to go shopping again. I couldn't possibly go back home without taking my family something from New York.

"Tina, could I see you for a minute?" I asked as I walked by her desk.

"Sure thing, Rachel, just give me a second."

In my office, I began to wrap things up. I still had several calls to make on behalf of my clients, I reminded myself as I went to my file cabinet and pulled some accounts. I had planned on working on them throughout the week, but since I'd be leaving soon I decided to get done as much as I could that day. I hated to leave any of my clients for someone else to be responsible for, because my own work ethic was high. That was the reason people asked for me, I never left them hanging.

"So you're going to Tucson!" Tina said as she entered my office.

"Yes, Tina, that was one of my messages that you gave me when I came in this morning. Reginald told me a little bit about it on the phone, but said he couldn't give me the particulars when he saw me in person. I was kind of excited about this assignment though. I think that I need a little getaway."

"You are married to your job," Tina said, shaking her head at me. "But it seems like this time you can mix a little business with pleasure."

"I just prefer working vacations," I said as I smiled at Tina.

"You're a workaholic Rachel," Tina cautioned. "What did you need me to do for you?"

"Oh, I really need your help. There is no way I can get all the work done and be ready by Thursday morning. Can I give you half of my files to fax? If you can do that for me, I can do the rest. Can you also make my calls return calls? And then I still have four letters I have to send out. I was going to start on another assignment, but it will have to be given to someone else," I explained in a hurry.

"Rachel, just give me all of the files. You just concentrate on your letters and your phone calls."

"Tina, are you sure?"

"Sure I'm sure. I'll fax them all off as soon as we get back from lunch. We are still on, aren't we?"

I can make it now."

"Great. I have several airline arrangements to make. I'll get all of that done before lunch so I can concentrate on your stuff afterward. Just let me know who needs what and where it's to be sent."

"Oh, and Tina, could you —"

"I know, I know. Make the necessary follow-up calls on your behalf to make sure they received everything, and ask if there's anything else we can do for them," Tina said as she stood to leave.

"You're a lifesaver," I told her.

"You know that I'm here for you, girl. Let me know if there is anything else I can do."

"Thanks Tina."

"Don't mention it. See you at lunch," Tina said as she left my office.

I was busy with all the work I needed to do. I had an hour and a half to make a dent in my workload before I had to meet Tina and Michelle for lunch in our usual lunch spot, Grimaldi's. It was located near the waterfront in Brooklyn and now the legendary Grimaldi's offered excellent pizzas. Cooked in a brick oven, the crusts emerge crispy and pleasantly charred. The toppings always consisted of only the freshest ingredients, including their delectable sausage, vegetables and mozzarella cheese. They also offered great soups and sandwiches.

Nearly two hours later, I headed over to Grimaldi's to meet Michelle and Tina. When I arrived, Tina had already found us seats close to the window and had saved one for me.

"So, I hear you're going to Tucson," Michelle said sullenly. "I've never been able to get a job that pays me to travel all over the world. Even Tina here gets to travel sometime."

"And did you hear the ranch has a spa on it?" Tina said teasingly with a childish smile on her face.

Michelle it's all work-related," I explained. "Though I do plan on getting a little relaxation and some sightseeing in, but that will be after I'm finished with work."

"Rachel, you're so committed to your job, I hope you really get some rest in," Tina told me.

I'll give you that, you are a hard worker," Val added. But you suck with men because you won't get with the one you need to be with."

"All right now Val, don't start."

"Don't start what? You know that Romey is going to divorce that floozy don't you? Then you two can get together."

"Val, that's not my goal."

"I know, but I'm just hoping for you. You know you need a good man, even if you won't admit it." Val said.

"You sound like my mother Val."

I do hope that you will meet you a really nice man who can take your mind off work at least for a little while," Tina added softly.

"Not you too Tina?"

"Well, maybe it's time you listened to us."

I rolled my eyes. "What do they have good to eat today?" I asked my friends.

"You know I always get my usual, a grilled tuna sandwich, and as usual it's great. Want a bite?" Val offered.

"No, I just can't make my mind up. I'll be right back," I told my friends.

I left the table and Val and Tina continued on with their lunch.

"Val, why do you ride her back so about finding a man? She will in her own time," Tina said.

"It's obvious she's lonely. The only thing she has in her life is this job and you and me."

"Well, she says that it's enough for her."

"Tina, you have Jessie and your kids. I have Trina and an occasional boyfriend or two. Rachel has two girlfriends that she meets up with every Friday night and for lunch at work. How much life is that for her? Even that thing she had with Chris finally blew up."

"It's not a life, but you know she wants to get ahead in her career. It doesn't matter. Whatever she does, it's got to be her choice. She's smart and funny, she's beautiful, and —"

"And she's not getting any younger. Tina, she's thirty years old. Her looks aren't going to hold up forever, you know."

"Well, maybe never having married or having kids would be all right for Rachel. We can't push her into a relationship."

"No, we can't," Mama replied. "But we can try."

"We'll argue about this later. Here she comes."

"Did you find something good?" Mama asked me.

I sat down in my seat. "I got the chicken noodle soup. Nothing else appealed to me. Hey, girls, I want to leave on Thursday for Chicago and then go on to Tucson. I want to leave as early as possible. I'll only have three days to visit my family. I have to leave Sunday for Tucson."

"Your mama is a sweetheart. Tell her I said hello," Mama said.

"I will."

"You know, you can bring her to New York again on your way back home," Mama added.

"I can see your evil plot brewing right now Mama. You would love to get together with my mother and match make."

"Who, me?" Mama said coyly.

"Well, I don't think I'll be able to bring her back anyway."

"Why? Mama asked.

"Because Reginald says that I will definitely be out there for a week or two. After that, it's up to me, but I have to be back for the grand opening."

"Why don't you take her out there for the grand opening?" Tina asked.

"At first I was thinking about it. She was even hinting around that she would like to come. I just know that she would start husband hunting, and since I really have to work I didn't think it would be a good idea."

"Rach, she only has your best interest at heart. We all do," Val told me.

"I know. I just want things to happen when they happen and when it feels right to me."

"Ladies, it looks like we're running low on time," Tina said as she glanced at her watch. "If I am going to get my work and your work done, I'd better get back."

"Thanks again for your help, Tina."

"Don't mention it."

I went straight to my office. I made all the phone calls and finished up the files I couldn't pass on to Tina.

I became momentarily lost in thought. I sat quietly thinking about Robin and Donnie. My sister met Donnie O'Neal during her second year of law school. Donnie was in his last year of law school and had a promising career as an attorney. With several law firms already interested in him, Donnie would go on to pass the bar on his first try. Right after he started working with Guni, Mouser, & Havner, he and Robin were married and she never finished law school. Robin would reason that two high-powered careers such as theirs would be devastating to the marriage she wanted to create. But I felt as though Robin's getting pregnant right after the wedding was the real reason.

They did have a happy marriage, I thought. My sister was always e-mailing me pictures of her kids. The little family had two boys and one girl. Donnie Jr. was the oldest at eight; Nikki was five and had just started kindergarten; Charles was the baby at only three. Robin certainly seemed content, but I couldn't understand how my sister could have so easily given up her dream of being an attorney. I knew that I certainly couldn't give up her job for a man. I could only think of all the times Robin and I would sit and talk about all the wonderful vacations they would take together when they both finished school. Then Donnie came along, and all the plans and dreams seemed to be forgotten by my sister.

I came back from daydreaming and said aloud, "That won't happen to me." I grabbed my purse and headed out the door.

I hailed a taxi and just as I got into the car I realized I had forgotten my laptop. "I don't know what's wrong with me. I need to get away more than I think." I signed. I made a mental note to remember to get it when I went into the office in the morning. Right now, I wanted to get home and make a phone call.

At home, I quickly took a shower. I figured out what to have for dinner later as it was till early. After I dried off, I picked up the phone and called my mother. It rang several times and I was just about to hang up when I heard a man's voice answer.

"Hi, Daddy," I said in an excited tone. "It's Rachel."

"Hey, baby girl, how are you?" he said, glad to hear from his daughter.

"I'm fine," I answered, happy to hear his familiar "baby girl" again. He had sweet pet names for Robin and me. When we were growing up, he had even called all their girlfriends sweet pea, or precious, nut baby girl belonged solely to me.

"I was calling to let you know that I am coming home for a long weekend."

"When will you get here?"

"Thursday morning, but I can only stay for three days, " I explained.

"I can pick you up at the airport. Do you know what time your flight will arrive?"

"Not yet. All of the plans for this trip are coming together this morning. I have to leave for Tucson, Arizona, Sunday morning."

"Business trip?"

"Yeah, but I'm trying to get in a little family time before I go there. I have an assignment to do some public relations work for a new ranch. I have to stay for two weeks, but after that I'm not due back there until the grand opening."

"So that's what your mother was talking about. It sounds like she would like to join you, but instead of just enjoying herself she would be busy husband hunting," my dad said knowingly.

"Bingo! And that's why I really don't want her to come. This job is really important to the firm. I need to concentrate on my job, not finding a man."

"I can understand that baby girl. You don't want to be pressured into a relationship right now, but you know that you're not getting any younger," he said sympathetically.

"I know that Dad. There is always a chance that I will never marry. I'm not going to marry just anyone to satisfy everyone else, and I certainly am not going to marry before I'm finished doing what I want to do with my life. I don't want to end up like Robin."

"Rachel, don't get upset. I guess we all just worry about you. We want to make sure that someone will take care of you."

"Daddy, I think I've proven time after time that I am quite capable pf taking care of myself," I said flatly.

"I've got to give you credit, you have proven that. Just make sure that I see more grandkids, okay, baby girl?"

"We'll see, Daddy. I have to call you back tomorrow with my flight information. Do you remember Tina, my secretary?"

"I sure do. I remember the fabulous meal she cooked at your place when we came up to visit," he said, making me laugh.

"Well, she'll probably give you a call with my flight information if you don't hear from me. Hey, where's Mama? I better say hello to her before I hang up."

"She's not home right now. She went over to Robin's to see the kids. Do you want me to have her call you back when she gets in?"

"No, that's okay. I'll just talk to her later," I said quietly. "I have to go, Daddy. I love you and I'll see you soon."

"Bye, baby girl. I love you."

I hung up the phone and sat on the sofa lost in thought. Once again I doubted myself. According to everyone I knew I was going to end up being some pitiful old maid, with an empty life. Didn't anyone understand that right now I was content with my life? How could I be happy? Everyone I knew was convinced that I was missing out on something special.

I wasn't completely unaware of how every time my mom and dad mentioned how happy Robin was being a wife and mother, I felt so forgotten and empty inside.

I tried to push the thought from my mind. I called my building's management office to let them know that I will be on an extended business trip.

Feeling a little hungry, I made myself a sandwich. I sat at my kitchen table in silence, noticing my apartment felt lonely and cold. Thoughts of Robin playing with her kids floated in my head. For the life of me, I couldn't figure out what was going on in my head.

Chapter

18

I woke Monday morning a little before five A.M. and shut off the alarm. Quickly dressing, I hurried down to the fitness center. When I arrived, my neighbor Lina was over in one area of the room running on the treadmill.

"Hey Rachel, how's everything?" Lina said.

"Just fine, how's that sweet little baby girl of yours?" I asked her, smiling.

"She's growing more beautiful every day," she said.

"I usually get in here and get a quick workout before I head to work. I'd better get a move on." I said quickly glancing at the wall clock.

"I better get going myself. I have to get to work also and drop Bebe off at the sitter. I'll see you around."

I finished my workout and went back to my apartment, showered and dressed for work.

"Good morning, Rachel," Tina said, from behind her desk.

"Good morning, Tina. How are the arrangements coming along?" I asked her.

"You're just about ready. Your plane tickets are being picked up by the courier, and do you see the little stack of files right there?"

"Yes?"

"That's all that is left of the pile you gave me to take care of," Tina said proudly.

"Oh, Tina, as always, I owe you big."

"No, you don't. Just remember to tell your family I said hello, especially your dad."

"I called him the other night. He was raving about your cooking. Oh, just in case I forget, could you call him and let him know my flight information?"

"I sure will."

I'll be in my office if you need me," I said as I headed down the hall.

"Are we on for lunch, or are you leaving early?"

"I'm leaving right after lunch. I'll see you and Val then."

I finished the last of the files in my office and made a few phone calls to my clients. I put my laptop next to my purse, which reminded me to check my email. I replied to all of my messages and then went back to Tina's desk.

"Tina, if you're finished, I can file those before we head out to lunch."

"Do you need any help?" Tina said as she handed me the stack of files.

"No. I'll be quick, and I'll meet you and Val at Grimaldi's," I said.

"Sounds good to me. Oh, the file on top is for you to take with you to Tucson. I compiled some information from the web about the area. I thought it might be useful."

"I'll put it with my laptop. Thanks, Tina, for everything," I said.

I went back to my office and filed the last of my client's information. Then I grabbed my purse and my laptop and went to meet Tina and Val.

When I got to Grimaldi's, they had just bought their food and wee looking for a seat. Finally, they found a table and sat down.

"Rachel, are you all ready for your trip?" Val asked.

"Yes, I am. You know, I think one day we all need to take a vacation together," I told them.

Val's face lit up until Tina's voice of reason dimmed it. "You know that the firm couldn't run properly with both of us gone."

"We could go for a long weekend or something," I told them.

"That would be great. I sure could use a vacation," Val said anxiously.

"Are you coming in tomorrow?"

"No. I'm going to pack tonight and shop tomorrow. I'll give you both a call before I leave town," I said and leaned over and gave my friends a good-bye kiss on the cheek. Tina and Val were like sisters to me. I would miss them terribly, especially our standing Friday night date.

I was headed home and decided to stop and pick up a bottle of wine. I wanted to relax, listen to music, pack, and if I was lucky, get a good night's rest.

After picking up the wine, I stopped by the Fausto Nieves Botanica, an aromatherapy & candle store and bought several scented candles. I felt as though I wanted to ensure that I had a relaxing, wonderful evening and night.

Unlocking the door of my apartment, I entered and set my laptop and purse on the sofa. I put the bottle of wine in the fridge to chill before looking around the apartment, trying to decide where I wanted to place my candles.

I opened the solid mahogany armoire and turned on my favorite jazz CD on the stereo. Then I went into the bedroom and put on a comfy pantsuit that I enjoyed lounging in and went to work packing.

Opening my suitcases, I packed, making a conscious effort not to forget my makeup or any of my other essentials. When I was done, I had four large suitcases. I wanted to call Tina and Val, but I wouldn't; I would talk to them tomorrow.

The bottle of wine had chilled, so I poured a glass and lay across the sofa and watched the movie *Two Can Play That Game*, holding the brochure on resort at Tucson. I lay there and watched the movie and drank my wine until I feel asleep.

When I awoke, it was morning. I turned off the television and went into the kitchen to make breakfast. I decided not to workout this morning, so I sat at the table sipping my coffee slowly and thinking about my trip. I had an interesting and exciting assignment ahead of me and looked forward to it.

I showered and dressed, grabbed my purse and keys and left. I had a lot of shopping to do before I went to visit my family in Chicago.

First, I went to Jim Hanley's Universe to buy some nice toys for my nephews and niece. Donnie Jr. was deeply interested in rare comics, especially the mini comics. This was a very good store because they specialize in hard to find comics, especially minis. I think they have more mini comics than any store I have ever been to. They also have a huge selection of statues, busts, t-shirts and toys. All of their stuff is reasonably priced for midtown Manhattan. They have sales, which is unheard of in comic book shops. They had a Superman Birthday sale where ALL Superman related items are 1/2 price. The staff is nice and loves to talk comics. I bought my beautiful niece books and a doll to add to the collection I had given her. My baby nephew was still very easily impressed. I bought him a battery-operated fire truck with all of the bells and whistles.

I went to Macy's for my mother and bought her a dress with all of the accessories. My dad was the easiest of all to shop for and would want his usual, some great smelling cigars from Hoboken Cigars, the only place that carried the brand they I wanted.

It was almost time for dinner when I finished with my shopping, and I was getting hungry. Knowing that I had nothing good at home, I decided to go to Peter Luger's Steakhouse.

"How many are in your party?" the maitre d' asked, shortly after I walked in.

"Just me," I answered and was quickly ushered to a table. I sat down and looked around the room. I was the only one sitting alone. There was a family across form me, two couples to my right, another behind me. I wasn't sure if the two men to my left were a couple or not, but I felt awkward sitting alone. When the waitress returned for take my order, I asked for a take-out menu instead. I ordered rib eye steak with mashed potatoes and went home.

Outside my door were the plane tickets Tina had sent to my apartment by courier. I ate quietly in my apartment, and then finished my packing before calling Tina.

"Hello," my friend answered.

"Hey, Tina, it's just me. How was work today?"

"It was fine, but not the same without you girlfriend. Are you all ready for your trip?"

"I think so. I got all of my shopping done, and I got the plane tickets, thank you."

"I just wanted to check in with you. I'd better go. I have to be up early tomorrow to catch that flight." I said.

"Okay, I'll talk to you later, Rachel. Have a safe trip."

"See you later."

Chapter 19

In the morning, I put all of my suitcases and laptop next to the door so that I wouldn't forget them. My laptop and purse would be the only two things that I will carry on the plane. Thank God my father would be there to pick me up at the airport, I thought. I had no idea how else I would be able to manage my entire luggage.

I made a pot of coffee and drank it slowly as I got dressed. I curled my hair with a curling iron and put on my makeup, and then I put on a pair of white cotton walking shorts, with matching top. I finished the rest of my coffee with a bagel with cream cheese, and then brushed out my soft curls allowing them to frame my face.

Frank, who was the limo driver who was supposed to take me to the airport, rang the doorbell just as I placed my dishes in the sink. I asked him to help me out with my luggage. I quickly checked myself one last time in the mirror and put my necessities in my purse.

The two of us made our way out to his parked limo and he placed all of my suitcases into the trunk; then he opened the door for me.

A half hour later, he pulled up in front of United Airlines.

"How did you know what airline I was taking?" I asked him curiously.

"Ms. Swanigan told me," he said with a wink.

"I should have known that Tina was on top of everything."

"She also told me to give you this," Frank said as he gave me a newspaper and an umbrella. I laughed; it was a joke between Tina and I. It seemed whenever the two us got caught in the rain, only one of us had an umbrella and the other had to use a newspaper.

At the gate, I had a twenty-minute wait before my plane started boarding. I was happy to be on my way to Chicago and was anxious to see my family. Hopefully, I would get to have some alone time with my sister Robin. I knew that my sister had a pretty full life, but I wondered if I would be able to steal her away from her family for one night. It had been a year since we had spent any time together, and I missed Robin more than I cared to admit.

Finally, my flight was called to board, and I was happy to be on my way, but I was also thankful that no one would be sitting beside me in first class. After the plane took off, I placed my purse and laptop holder in the vacant seat as

I clicked away on my computer, writing some letters that I would need to send out once I landed. Next, I opened the folder Tina had given me with the information she had researched on Tucson. Since I had never been to Arizona, I read the information thoroughly: I figured it would be useful to know a little about the place I would be visiting.

As I read, I grew more excited about Tucson. The area was rich in Native American history, which interested me, since my great-great grandfather was from the Sinagua tribe. I read on, making mental notes to rent a car and visit Sedona.

Tina knew about my Sinagua heritage from our talks and she had included some information about their culture. I learned that Sedona is located twenty-seven miles south of Flagstaff on AZ 89A. The area encompasses some 500 square miles of central Arizona and its regions are divided into Red Rock Country, Oak Creek Canyon, and greater Sedona. This Native American culture is alive and well in present-day Sedona. Visitors can inevitably share their long-established reverence for the land. Just as they hold many places around Sedona to be sacred, travelers will doubtlessly find their reverence to be well placed. There are many fine examples of Native American artistry in Sedona's galleries and shops. Native American pottery and jewelry are some of the most popular items for visitors. However, Native American music and dance are often showcased at various venues and all interested parties should consider booking one of Sedona's Native American tours to visit the sites and learn more about the historic people of this region. Travelers would thrill to view the ancient past that is preserved on the walls of Sedona's rocks. Woo Canyon's pictograph panel was a well-preserved example of the ancient Native art that showed pictographs of people and animals. Woo Canyon is an offshoot of Red Canyon that is about a half mile south of the Palatka site. Sedona's largest cliff dwelling was called Honanki and was presumably constructed by the Southern Sinagua roughly eight hundred years ago.

"Would you like something to drink?" the flight attendant asked me.

I looked up from my reading and asked for a Sprite. Thanking the attendant for the drink, I turned and stared out of the window. I still hadn't overcome the excitement I felt about the assignment.

I returned to my reading and saw that there were lots of activities to keep me busy. I wouldn't mind visiting Tombstone. I loved the movie *Tombstone* and Tombstone Arizona is perhaps most famous for its Gunfight at OK Corral when the Earp brothers, Wyatt, Virgil and Morgan, along with friend Doc Holliday shot it out with the Clanton and McLaury Gang. The fierce gunfight was quick and when the bullets stopped flying, Billy Clanton, Tom McLaury and Frank McLaury lay dead. Billy's brother Ike Clanton kept his life that day, but was eventually murdered near Springerville

Arizona. Virgil and Morgan Earp needed weeks to recover from serious wounds, but Doc Holliday was barely grazed by a bullet. Surprisingly, Wyatt Earp was unscathed.

I definitely have to visit Old Tucson Studios because it was Arizona's Hollywood in the desert. It was voted "Best Western Movie Set" by True West Magazine and listed among five one-of-a-kind Tucson sites in USA Today. Passing through the gates of an old frontier town, visitors from around the globe are transported back to a time when fearless men with six shooters ruled the Old West. Saunter down the streets of Hollywood's most famous movies; walk in the footsteps of movie legends like John Wayne, Clint Eastwood and hundreds more. In addition to its historic role as a film location, Old Tucson Studios is Southern Arizona's premier outdoor entertainment venue with a full array of live shows, thrilling stunts, Old West dramas, saloon musicals, trail rides and fun for the whole family.

There is one more place I would like to visit and it is Tempe Town Lake. Imagine an urban environment where you could spend the morning sailing across crystal clear lake waters, picnicking on grass knolls or strolling along smooth sandy beaches, followed by an afternoon concert at an outdoor amphitheater, with dinner at dozens and dozens of restaurants or cafés within walking distance. Even better, imagine not even having to drive to this urban refuge as you board the light rail from the station nearest your home and you glide quickly over the rails to alight effortlessly at your destination. For those living in the Phoenix area, this imagined oasis is just Valents away at *Tempe Town Lake*. More than just a city waterside park, *Tempe Town Lake* is a civic masterpiece of open Two miles in length and found along the traditional banks of the normally dry *Salt* River, Tempe Town Lake combines innovative design with the wonders of nature into a vibrant mix of outdoor recreation, arts and culture settings, premier retail shops and fine dining. Completed in the 1990s after two decades of planning, design and engineering challenges, today Tempe Town Lake is the crown jewel of the City of Tempe and provides a destination experience for not only those nearly 1,000,000 people living within ten miles of the Lake, but over 4,000,000 in the Momley of the Sun. Town Lake runs from just east of Mill Avenue west to about Curry Road and along Rio Salado Parkway in the heart of downtown Tempe. Town Lake's *Beach Park,* considered by many to be the town's finest special event space, borders the *Historic Mill Avenue District.* Here visitors can enjoy exciting nightclubs, dine in the finest Tempe restaurants or find that perfect gift item at nearly 200 shops brought together in the unsurpassed mix of businesses that only the Mill Avenue District can offer. Nearby *Arizona State University,* home to *Sun Devil Stadium,* is within walking distance and forms a stunning backdrop for visitors strolling along the shores or enjoying a paddle cruise across the water.

I quickly remembered how I had felt at Peter Luger's Steakhouse, surrounded by all the couples, and I knew to steer clear of the little romantic inns. I really didn't need that heartache right now.

When the captain announced that they were approaching the Chicago O'Hare International Airport, I put my laptop and file back in their bag, tucked them under the seat in front of me, and fastened my seat belt.

After I exited the plane, I grabbed a luggage cart and walked toward the baggage claim area. I waited patiently for my luggage to arrive. When it did, I collected all of my bags and placed them on the cart, and then headed for the main entrance. Once outside, I looked around trying to spot my parents' car. I could see my father waving to me and I started walking in his direction.

"How was your flight baby girl," he asked, obviously happy to see me, as he kissed my cheek.

"It was fine Daddy. Were you here long?"

"Not at all. Tina called to let me know what time to be here, and said she would call if there were any changes in your arrimom time. I told her that she didn't have to do that, but she insisted. Since I didn't hear from her, I assumed your flight would arrive on schedule."

"She has really been great. She helped to pull this trip together fast for me, and even handled some of my office work. I don't know what I would do without her."

"I can believe that. I still think that you should have brought her with you. I sure could use some of her cooking. Not that your mother is bad, I just like that good old Louisanna cooking she does."

"Where's Mama?" I asked.

"She's circling around because she didn't want to park," he answered as he looked around to see if he could see his wife. "Here she comes now," he said as he signaled to her.

My mom pulled up to the curb and got out. She ran over and gave her youngest daughter a big hug. "Oh, Rachel, you're finally here. I'm so happy to see you!"

"I'm happy to see you too Mom," I said, smiling.

My father put the suitcases into the trunk while my mother and I greeted each other.

As my father pulled into the driveway, I saw Robin's kids playing in the yard. I smiled at them as they all ran toward the car. As soon as I got out, two children calling out my name that was extremely excited about seeing me surrounded me. I bent down and gave each a big kiss.

"Hi, sis!" Robin said as she came out of the house to greet me. Though she had baby Charles in her arms, she managed to give me a hug. "It's good to see you."

"It's good to see you, too. I missed you. Email doesn't have anything on seeing you in the flesh," I said as my sister led me into the house. Donnie Jr. helped his granddad carry in my luggage.

Inside, my family and I gathered in the dining room where Robin had prepared a wonderful lunch of fried chicken, potato salad, baked beans, and lemonade. My family ate and asked me many questions about Manhattan and my new job assignment in Tucson.

"Rachel, how long will you be in Tucson?" Robin asked.

"Initially, I'll be there for about two weeks. After that, I'll just have to play it by ear until the grand opening."

"You have such an exciting job," Robin stated.

"For the most part, I do love my career and one of the perks is getting to travel to wherever my job-related business takes me," I said smiling confidently.

I decided to interrupt the question and answer cycle by giving the kids the gifts I had bought.

"Donnie, do you think you are strong enough to pull the big suitcase over here to me?" I asked my oldest nephew.

"Auntie Rachel, please," he said as he stood and rolled up his sleeve. "Look at this," he said, showing me his pretend muscle.

"Wow!" I said in mock surprise. "Have you been working out?"

"I sure have," he said, with a wide smile on his face, happy I had noticed. Donnie pulled the suitcase toward me and then sat back down.

"This is for you, Donnie," I said, and handed him the stack of comic books. "Are you sure into the Superman comics?" I asked him.

"Yes! Thanks, Auntie Rachel!" he gave me a big hug and kiss.

"What did you bring me, Auntie Rachel?" Nikki asked anxiously.

"Oh Nikki, you know that I didn't forget my sweetheart," I said. Reaching into the suitcase, I brought out a big doll. Nikki grabbed it squeezed it tight.

"I love her!" Nikki said. "I love you too, Auntie Rachel," my little niece said, hugging me, before she ran to her mother to show her the doll.

I watched my sister as she looked at the doll I had given her daughter. She paid close attention to everything her little girl was saying. Sensing my eyes on her, Robin looked up.

"Rachel, you're a wonderful auntie," Robin said, making me smile.

"This is for Charles," I said as I handed the fire truck and the books I had bought for the kids to my sister.

"Mom, this is for you," I said as I handed her a package. "I hope that you like it," I added.

"Rachel, it feels like Christmas when you come home," my mom said with a smile. She opened her package and saw the beautiful dress with all of the accessories. "Oh, Rachel, this is lovely. The color is beautiful. Thank you, sweetheart," she told me as she leaned over and kissed my cheek.

"Daddy, there's no surprise in what I got you. You know that your gift is your usual," I said walking over to him.

"Thanks, baby girl. I knew you wouldn't let me down." I handed my father two boxes of his favorite cigars. He took one out and smelled it. "Ah, I'll save this one for after dinner," he announced as he stuffed it into his shirt pocket.

"Robin, I couldn't decide on what to get James and you, so I thought that I might keep the kids one night and let you two have some private face time."

"Rachel, that's a wonderful idea. Are you certain that you want to do that — I mean, to take on these three?"

"Sure. It will be fun and it will give me a chance to spend some quality time with my niece and nephews. Besides, Big Donnie here can help me out with the little one," I said, smiling at my nephew. He smiled back, happy to be considered so mature.

"Rachel, your room is ready if you want to get settled in," my mom said.

"I guess that I would like to freshen up a bit, but first, I'll help clean up."

"No, don't worry about. I got this sweetheart," my mother said carrying some dishes to the sink. Robin, you help your sister with her suitcases," she added.

Robin and I made our way upstairs, each one with a suitcase in our hand. I cautiously balanced my purse and laptop in the other hand.

"I'll go and get the other suitcase," Robin said.

"Thanks sis. I'll start unpacking," I said.

Robin left the room and returned momentarily with my last suitcase and placed it in the corner with the others before sitting down on the bed.

"You still have an amazing figure," Robin told me as I slid on a pair of jeans. "What are you, a size four?"

"No, I'm a six. You don't look bad yourself, Robin."

"Thanks. Flattery will get you everywhere."

"You've got to remember now that you have had three kids and you're in great shape. What are you, a size eight?" I asked, giving my sister the one-over.

"I'm a nine but I may be at an eight by the time I see you again little sister. I'm going to start trying to walk everyday. Walking is easily the most popular form of exercise. It burns approximately the same amount of calories per mile as does running, a fact particularly appealing to those people like me who find it difficult to sustain the jarring effects of long distance jogging."

"Let's do something together tonight while I'm here," I suggested.

"Just us two?" Robin asked.

"Yes, just the two of us. I know who can keep the kids for a while. Let's go shopping or go to the movies."

"What makes you think Mom will keep the kids?" Robin asked.

"Take note big sister and watch me in action," I said, as I slipped on a different blouse.

Mother was sitting in the floor playing with Nikki, and our father was still sitting in his chair.

"Mom, would you like to spend some time with the kids? Robin and me would like to have a little time together before I have to leave."

"Tonight, Rachel?" my mother asked, trying to hide her shock.

"Tonight would be perfect, thanks Mama," I said excitedly as I bent down to kiss her. I grabbed my sister's hand and said, "We won't be out late. Bye."

"Thanks, Mama," Robin said, grabbing her purse and car keys.

Robin and I said nothing until we pulled off, then we burst into laughter.

Robin and I skipped the movies and decided on going to Woodfield Mall. Just 30 minutes outside of Chicago,

Woodfield Mall is home to almost 300 stores and averages 50,000 visitors a day. One of the busiest malls in the world, Woodfield is a must for serious shopaholics.

After Robin and I had our fill of shopping, we went to the New Checkerboard Lounge for Blues 'n' Jazz. This legendary South Side music hang in Hyde Park's Harper Court mall no doubt had top-notch blues and jazz musicians--both well-knowns and newbies, and they will continue to grace the stage. Expect a crowd that's a mix of University of Chicago students, Hyde Park locals, music lovers and fans of the original Checkerboard. A spacious bar and seating area with checkerboard motif create a cozy community feel where you can kick back and listen to the music. Robin and I could listen to live jazz, get a drink, and chat it up for a while before going back home.

My sister and me really enjoyed our night out. We talked more about my job because I could tell that Robin was truly interested in it. Robin and I had always been pretty close and I always knew that she accepted me just the way I am. She didn't push me to find a man, or play any games. Robin was Robin, accepting, loving, and nurturing. Even when I was dreaming of a career in public relations and moving to New York, it was Robin who had supported me.

I thanked Robin for her love and acceptance. Sometimes people would treat me like there's something wrong with me because I'm not married. But I'm pretty happy with my life and if I wasn't happy with it, I wouldn't get married just to please everybody.

I loved my big sister. Just like when we were small, Robin had a way of making everything all right, or at the least it seemed right. It was my mother who made me feel like a failure, for not being married with children like Robin.

Robin and I looked at some more of the shops before they closed. My sister enjoyed it more than me because she didn't get a lot of opportunities to get out of the house without the kids and I felt that she was trying to get in as much time as possible. We really weren't shopping as much as we were enjoying each other's company.

Robin bought me a beautiful glass bluebird. She told me to never let anyone tell you what your dreams are; always be happy knowing you're making the right decision for you.

Robin and I decided we'd better go home. Mama was probably all played out by now I thought, remembering the trick I had played on my mother.

When we reached our parents' home, it was nine-thirty in the evening. Robin gathered up her kids and said goodnight before going home. I helped my mother straighten up the living room. When my mom took a couple of glasses into the kitchen, I made a quick call. My mother came out just as I finished talking and said that she was going to bed and asked if I needed anything. Since I was okay, she told me that she was going to bed.

I went upstairs to my room and changed into my nightgown and lay down in bed. In my room, which was illuminated by the moonlight, I couldn't stop thinking about my sister Robin. *Robin*. I used to hold so much animosity against her. I had been jealous of how my mother had always made it seem that Robin was so wonderful for getting married and having children. My mother would go on and on to anyone who would listen about the wonderful life "Robin" had.

I thought long and hard, and couldn't remember a time when my mother had carried on so about her. Even so, I shouldn't have harbored resentment toward my sister for how my mother made me feel. Just like tonight, Robin was there for me, letting me know that I was perfect just the way I was. My sister had never failed to let me know that she was always in my corner. I had come to realize that I adorned my sister, and having made peace with that insecurity, I fell asleep with a smile on my face.

Chapter 20

Sunday morning had arrived, and to my surprise, I wasn't ready to leave my family. My visit with my family was brief but I enjoyed it so much. I sat on the bed and looked out of the window of what used to be my room. I remembered the many times Robin and me exchanged secrets and sat up into the wee hours talking about everything.

I gathered my purse, laptop, and suitcase and went downstairs. My father was already waiting in the living room.

"Good morning, baby girl," he said sadly.

"Daddy, please don't look like that," I said as I gave him a long hug.

"How else am I supposed to look? My baby girl is leaving again, and I'm not happy about that. I'm going to miss you like crazy Rachel."

"I'll be back before you know it," I said, still wishing I didn't have to go.

I ate breakfast with my parents and enjoyed great conversation. My mother gave me two letters and told me that they were not to be opened until after I had gotten on the plane. One of the letters was from Robin and the other from Donnie Jr. I knew that if I read them now, I would cry and I just didn't want to cry in front of my dad.

A calm seemed to come over us as we sat there in the kitchen. My parents exchanged glances, realizing that they would not be seeing their daughter for a good while. But mostly I think that my parents just weren't ready to see me go. I reassured them that they would see me again as soon as summer. When I told them that, their moods seemed to lift a little.

Mom and Dad took me to the airport. As I prepared to leave to my parents, I could feel my heart breaking. I waved good-bye and walked inside the airport. A little later, I was ushered to first class. I placed my laptop in the overhead compartment, and then took my seat, placing my purse on the floor next to my feet. I removed the two letters from my purse expecting them to be very sad. Instead, their letters stated how much fun they both had with me and wished me a safe trip.

I placed the letters back into my purse and fastened my seatbelt. I could hear the roar of the planes' engines and the voice of the flight attendant resonating over the intercom. I sat and stared out of the window as the plane taxied down the runway.

At last, I was on my way to Tucson. I had felt anxious for the past week and thought that I could use the break from the rat race of New York. I secretly hope that I would get a chance to experience the spa's facilities because it was a long overdue relaxation. I had been so busy over the past few years getting my company off the ground and running that I never took time out for myself. I really was looking forward to some time for me while I'm in Tucson — a time to rejuvenate and revive.

Chapter 21

Having finished my assignment in Tucson, I returned home to the hustle and bustle of New York. The trip had given me renewed spirits and I felt revived and ready to take on the world again. Arizona is a spa lover's paradise, with some of the best spas in the country. My spa experience was one of tranquility and relaxation. There were elegantly appointed treatment rooms that offered a diverse menu of spa experiences that incorporated beautiful, tranquil settings and indigenous flora and fauna into signature treatments where ancient rituals join force with cutting-edge techniques. I was more than happy to put on a spa robe and sandals and relax using the steam, sauna and whirlpools. I was able to escape my fast-forward, mad, current world and had entered into a quieter place to recover, so that I could dive back into life again - energized.

I also got a chance to rent a car and visit Tempe Town Lake, Old Tucson Studios at Tombstone, and the place of my great-great granddads' ancestry — Sedona. I'd had a great time.

"Morning, Rachel," Tina said as I walked through the door. "I'm so happy that you're back. We had missed you so much," she added.

"I'm happy to see you too and to be back at the office, "I said smiling, as I reached into my shopping bag. "I brought you some souvenirs from Tucson," I added, handing Tina a beautifully wrapped gift box.

Tina hurriedly opened the box to find a beautiful Native American Indian bracelet and earring set.

"I love this Rachel, thank you."

"I wanted you to have something nice to show my appreciation for all the hard work you did helping me prepare for my trip and also because you are my friend Tina. I got Mom a set too."

"Thanks for the souvenirs Rachel and I know we are on for lunch as usual right?"

"You know girl," I said as I entered my office.

I had not been in my office for very long when my phone began ringing.

"Well, hello stranger," the masculine voice said at the other end of the phone. "How are you Rach?"

"Romey, gosh it's been a long time since we last talked," I replied. "Why hadn't you called me before now?"

"Well Rach, I was just trying to give you space. Also, I have been trying to deal with my own problems. You know that Frannie and I got divorced."

"I'm so sorry Romey. I'd hope that the two of you would eventually work through your differences."

For a moment, I thought to myself, *I'm glad that Frannie and Romey divorced. She had never really appreciated him. She had been one selfish, materialistic piece of work. It seems so obvious that she only cared about her possessions, money and social status, not to mention all the focus on vanity. Can Frannie not see that all of that is temporary because it could change in an instant? Momues are rare and people have less and less respect for the meaning of life. It's ok to have things, but to be driven by materialism is another story. I guess there will always be shallow people who are motivated by instant gratification, but to me, it really conceals a serious lack within the person.*

"Franchesca and I have been divorced for about six months now," Romey admitted, displaying a regretful expression on his handsome face.

"Mom had mentioned it to me before I went on my business trip."

"That's right. You went to Tucson didn't you?"

"Yes — and I got back last night. It was a good trip and I even got a chance to go to the spa. It was a wonderfully, relaxing experience."

"Yeah, you went there and they treated you like a queen and spoiled your ass," Romey said, being mock sarcastic of my experience.

"You keep talking like that and you won't be getting your souvenir I brought back for you," I said, with teasing attitude.

"Okay – okay! I apologize Rach. Hail to the Queen!" he said smiling broadly. "But seriously though, you deserved that great feeling and so much more," Romey said solemnly.

I got kind of quiet and a serious look formed on my face. I was going to tell Romey that Chris and I were through for good, not that anything would change between the two of us because of that. But we have always shared important milestones in our lives since we were kids. Though I still wished that there could be more between us, I have always cherished our friendship and I really didn't want to chance losing it by changing the status of our relationship from platonic to being lovers.

"Well, Chris and I are through for good this time."

"It's about time. That fool didn't deserve you anyway."

"I know Romey. I had to find out for myself."

"Well I say good rid dens to him and Franchesca. Who needs them anyway — we got us. You know what we can do — let's go out and celebrate our freedom. I'll treat you to dinner. Want to go?"

"Uh –h – h, well, I guess so. Why not? It shouldn't hurt that two good friends go out to dinner. Where would we go?"

"How about the Sequoia?"

"Sounds good to me."

"Do you want me to pick you up Rachel?"

My heart was saying yes, but instead I said, "I can meet you here say about six o'clock?"

"Cool, I'll see you then."

I was busy the rest of the day getting emails sent out to my clients and working on files. The day nearly passed in a blur, but I was more than ready to go by four o'clock that evening.

I made it home around four-thirty and I showered and put hot curlers in my hair. I selected a pair of cream-colored wide-legged trousers and matched them with a cream-colored silk top. After putting on my makeup, I dressed and put on a few dabs of my favorite fragrance — *Paul Sebastian's Casual.* I removed the curlers and brushed my hair up into an updo and allowed a few select curly tendrils to hang loosely. I had dressed with care for my dinner with Romey and almost felt like a schoolgirl getting ready to out on a date with her boyfriend. Romey probably didn't see me nor want me in that way, but that didn't mean I wasn't desirable … especially if I was foolish enough to want a man in my life. At least that's what I told myself until I strolled into the

Sequoia and saw Romey's handsome face. I looked hard for a hint of appreciation, if not desire, in his eyes.

"Hello Rachel," Romey greeted. "Wow! You look great!" he remarked as he pulled out a chair for me at the table.

I felt some disappointment because Romey's look seemed to only be appreciation, but I guess one out of two isn't bad.

Our table was in a quiet area of the restaurant as he'd requested, the service was impeccable, the food delicious. Or maybe everything was right because he was sitting across the table from me.

Little did I know that I would know how he had secretly felt about me and for how long in the very near future. I would soon know how beautiful I looked to him, how much that he wanted to tell me that, but couldn't in fear of making me become suspicious. Romey knew too well how smart I was and that I loved my independence. Romey had gotten angry each time he thought of Chris towering over me. Romey was the one — I just didn't know it yet, but Mom did. Romey had been confiding in Mom for a long time about how he felt about me, but he had sworn her to secrecy. I will learn later that this was why Mom could only suggest that I do certain things. If she had done anything more, it would betray Romey's confidence and make me suspicious.

After our dinner, Romey and I just sat at the table chatting. I could sense that it was something he wanted to say, but he seemed to not know how.

"You know Rachel, I have read all of your work — even back to your very first article, *Nice Guys Finish First*. I made a sort of scrapbook of you and your writing and have been keeping it up for years now. I love reading your articles. They're great," Romey said with much adoration.

"Really! Are you serious? I didn't know that you did that." I said smiling shyly. "I don't know of anyone who has done that Romey."

"You are such a smart, intelligent woman. Hey — you're my best friend."

Romey still showed signs of restlessness and I knew that he wanted to talk about something, so I decided to ask him.

"What's on your mind Romey," I asked concerned.

"I may have found someone to help me in getting a record deal. They loved the demo that I sent them and they're ready to offer me a deal. They want to sign me up Rach," he said flashing a brilliant smile.

"Romey, that's great news. I am so happy for you. I always knew that you would make it — I knew it," I shrieked running around the table to hug my friend, causing a few people to look around at us. "Now you did check them out, right?"

"Sure I did Rach. They are a legit record label — it's all good," he assured me.

"Now the offer still stands," I said walking back around the table to seat myself. I can write up a great article on you that will place you in the public eye. You know that I'm good at public relations."

"No Rach, you're great at public relations. I know because I have read all of your articles."

Looking at Romey, I could still see that something wasn't jiving with him and it had begun to concern me a bit.

"Your record deal isn't the only thing on your mind is it?"

"No Rach, it's not," he said with melancholy in his voice. I want to ask you something Rachel and I need for you to be completely honest with your answers, okay?"

"Sure, Romey."

"Do you believe that friends can be more than friends and make it?"

"What do you mean? I don't really understand what you are trying to ask me."

"Do you think that best friends can become perfect lovers?"

A knot formed in my throat and a wave of apprehension washed over me. I wondered where he might be going with this question. Clearing my throat, I tried to explain my thoughts on the subject.

"Romey, you know what — that is one of the most hotly debated questions about relationships. Do you know that question was famously posed in the film *When Harry Met Sally*: can men and women be just good friends? Well, according to the neurotic Sally, played by Meg Ryan, they can, but Billy Crystal's Harry insisted that platonic friendships are doomed because physical attraction always interferes. "Men and women can't be friends because the sex part always gets in the way," he says when they first meet."

"Rachel — I want to know what you think about friends becoming lovers," Romey insisted.

My body now trembled inside from apprehension but I swallowed hard and tried to give Romey an honest, heart-felt answer.

I –I'm kind of like Billy Crystal I guess Romey. I'm afraid that a love relationship might ruin a great friendship," I said, shocked at what I had just admitted. "Using the two of us as an example, I wouldn't want to lose our friendship, by risking it for love. What if love doesn't work, then what will we have?" I added.

"But generally speaking Romey, I think there was a survey done that was suppose to shatter Harry's cynicism by suggesting that friends who become lovers can maintain their friendship even if the sexual relationship breaks down. I'm not sure if I believe in that survey though. This website called *Friends Reunited,* polled about 2,000 people and found that only a third of friendships ended as a result of friends becoming lovers. More than eight in 10 of those questioned admitted that they were aware of the so-called "Harry met Sally syndrome" and feared that having sex with a friend would ruin the friendship. However, of those who had close friends of the opposite sex, 56 per cent of women and 65 per cent of men said they had considered taking the friendship to another level. And of the seven in 10 people who did, only a third said sex had destroyed the friendship. A third said they were still in the relationship and a third had returned to being good friends."

"But Rachel, it's just as likely that if it doesn't work out, you'll go back to just being friends. Best-friend dating makes sense to me because deep friendship is at the core of any longlasting romantic relationship," Romey stated.

There was something else I remembered reading at that website. Some people were asked why they had not dated a best friend and half of women said it was because they "just didn't fancy him" and a fifth said they feared it would destroy the friendship. Around a third of men and women shied away from romance with a best friend because "we just know each other too well. Some so-called experts remain divided over whether men and women can ever be just good friends. There was one lady that said she believed that friendship was an excellent foundation for a long-lasting relationship. She thought that friends have common momues and relationships work if they are built on common momues. I think that the problem is that many people get together on the basis of chemical attraction alone.

Then once the sex 'kicks out', they don't have anything left to maintain a friendship."

"Well, I still believe that it's possible for the relationship to work," Romey said. "Well, anyway, I got my answer. I appreciate your honesty Rach."

Sitting my glass on the table, I reached over and pulled Romey's hands into mine.

"We will find our true soul mates. We are just going through a bad patch right now." I said, trying to lift his spirits. "I had better go. Will you be all right Romey?"

"Uh - Uh – Yeah –sure Rach."

"Well, take care and I'll call you, " I said, with a playful wink.

After getting home, I felt absolutely horrible. I couldn't believe that I had said all of those things to Romey. He was trying to tell me that he wanted to be with me and I just shot him down. He was testing the waters trying to judge my reactions. Romey and I have had this long-standing friendship for so long and have had plenty of time to develop this bond. We already know that we have plenty in common and our judgement tends to be more reliable. I'd found this affable, gentle man very appealing as a shoulder to cry on when my succession of thrilling but chaotic relationships dissolved. He'd even sit with me once in the bar and had a couple of warm-up drinks while I waited for a new date to arrive. But then something changed and it happened quickly. Back then, everyone around me was saying how handsome and virile he was, and I suddenly thought they were right. It was like an epiphany. I guess I could sum it up as kind of like foreplay. All the time we were being friends, we were learning more about each other. Subconsciously I guess I was deciding whether I can take it further, from a friendship on to a more emotional and sexual level. Maybe Romey was right. Maybe friends can be great lovers.

My mind took me on a jouney into the abyss of love, friendship and relationships. My true thoughts on friends and lovers have been greatly altered after reading this writing by ~ StinaLisa ~. Her writing really touched me in ways that I never imagined. Her writing also expresses how I feel about being truly committed to someone. This was what I read: . . . *They are playmates, companions, and equal partners, as well as intimate and sharing lovers and confidants. They allow each other to be themselves within their own persona and uniqueness, and happily accept the other's good qualities and attributes. They display patience and understanding in the not-so-good qualities and innate character flaws, and allow the other to be less than "perfect."*

As friends and lovers, they encourage each other's individual growth, and are available for help and advice when needed. At the same time, they each sustain their own individual growth and feel free to ask for help and advice when needed from the other. If two people together can work on their individual growth, the growth between them can only become deeper. They desire a mutual growth in the entity of "two becoming one" to nourish and maintain a unified and intimate bonding.

Sensitivity, compassion, and a supportive nature are momuable assets to a lasting love. Special lovers offer support when needed, but also allow the other to experience the lessons they need to learn on their individual travels through life. Only through these lessons can they each become healthy and whole. They realize they cannot change at the will of another, but they can change for the improvement of themselves. This self-improvement can only lead to a deeper realization of a compatible and parallel relationship between them.

Fidelity and faithfulness are a "given" between friends and lovers. The sharing of two souls and two bodies are essential elements in the mystery of "love." To reach the ultimate highs and peaks of a very special love, this type of sharing can only be with each other.

Loving oneself has to come first before love for another can begin. It is only through self-love that a healthy relationship can survive. Two people cannot love each other at the expense of themselves, nor can they sacrifice or lose their identity and individualism for the other. If they did, their love would not prevail. They can, however, compromise and rearrange their lives to allow the other to become an intricate part of their life.

A satisfying love needs to be fed and nurtured. Like a beautiful garden, love needs healthy nourishment, for without it, it will surely fade and die. The love they share will be an unconditional love. They will love the other for the person they are, and not the person they want them to be. And they will always remember each other as the person with whom they fell in love. Money and things will never be objects of their love, for these material things have no substance. Material things come and go, but the love between two souls will last an eternity.

As lovers, they will carry the other within their hearts each day. A smile, a word, or a soft touch will be gentle memories that can be recalled whenever they are apart. Thoughts of their last moment together, whether it is a kiss, or the sweet melting of their bodies together, can nourish their time apart and hasten the need to return to each other's arms.

We all came into this world to discover who we are, and to pursue our created purpose. The one with whom we choose to share an intimate and sharing love is a very important element in gaining that knowledge. There is a special someone out there who is waiting for each of us and wanting the same. If we have prepared ourselves for the desires of our heart, and are patient in our endeavors, one day our paths will cross, and when this happens, we will recognize and know each other, for it is then that our souls will touch.

I had never thought about this moving article until now and it was causing me to have second thoughts about Romey and me. I was starting to believe that maybe he and I did stand a chance of making a go of it. Maybe I should go back and talk to him about it.

I grabbed my purse and keys and headed back to the Sequoia. As I parked my car, I saw Romey and Franchesca walking out of the restaurant together arm in arm. They seemed to be laughing and talking and enjoying each other so much. I watched as Romey gently placed his hand on her cheek as they intimately talked. After seeing Romey kiss her, I couldn't take anymore. I drove off with tears streaming down my face.

Nearly blinded my my tears, the drive home was in a blur but I did manage to get there safely. I undressed, put on my pajamas, and lay across my bed, totally saddened and heart-broken from seeing Romey with Frannie. I couldn't believe that I had been so weak as to believe that Romey and I could actually have something together. *What in the hell I was I thinking*, I scolded myself. *Well I'm not going to let it get the better of me*, I sniffed.

I pulled the covers back on my bed and crawled in. I grabbed one of my pillows and hugged it tightly as if I wasn't letting it go. I said to myself, *Rachel, tomorrow will be a new day. You will get up tomorrow and start everything new. You will not dwell in the past because you are a strong, independent woman. You have a wonderful career and company. Forget Roman Sinclair and the horse that he rode in on.*

Chapter
22

This morning I woke up with a mission on my mind — to throw myself into a project with everything that I had in me. I made a pot of coffee, poured me a cup and walked out on my terrance. Today was going to be a new beginning for me emotionally. I going to focus on other things in my life and move on.

Suddenly, I had a revelation. I had already done some indepth, thorough profiles on some of Motown's greatest artists such as, Diana Ross and the Supremes, Marvin Gaye, Stevie Wonder, The Four Tops, Smokey Robinson and the Miracles, The Jackson 5, The Temptations, Martha and the Vandellas, Mary Wells, The Marvelettes, Tammi Terrell, The Isley Brothers, Kim Weston, Jr. Walker and the All-Stars, Gladys Knight and the Pips, Rare Earth, The Commodores, Lionel Richie, Rick James, and many more. Why not pull it all together in a book and call it *Forever Motown*. This book will contain a collection of profiles on many record labels of the oldies era that I have compiled over the years. Since it has all been researched already, it would be very easy to create a book. I absolutely loved the idea and started to work on it immediately.   Between running my company and working on my book, I had very little time to think about Romey or Franchesca. I didn't care what they did anymore. That was Romey's little red wagon and he was the one who was going to have to pull it. I had taken myself out of the romance game and settled in on doing my own thing.

I started gathering up all of my material for the book I was going to write and set up a table next to my computer to organize everything. Just as I pulled out my chair to sit down at the computer, the doorbell rang. When I answered the door, there stood Mom.

"How are you doing sweetie?" she said smiling.

I turned and walked back into my apartment with Mom trailing behind me.

"Why are you so glum baby? What's wrong with you?"

"Nothing Mom," she said, shuffling around some papers on her desk.

"Well it sure doesn't seem like nothing to me. I called you last night, but I guess you were out or something. Where were you Rach?"

"I really don't want to talk about it Mom. It was so brain-less and dim-witted of me to think that —"

I stopped before I could finish my sentence. My mind flashed back to the conversation she and Romey had last night. He felt that they stood a chance at making a permanent transition from friends to lovers. In a weak moment, she had succumbed and allowed herself to believe that they could do it, but it had been short-lived.

"It was brain-less of you to think what Rachel? What in the world are you talking about? You lost me," Mom said, shrugging up her shoulders and displaying a look of uncertainty.

"Look Mom, I may as well tell you because you will dog me relentlessly until I do. I went out to dinner last night with Romey."

Mom's eyes lit up like a Christmas tree. She has always been on a crusade to get Romey and me together more than any of her other prospects and refused to totally give up him because he was her favorite.

"And," Mom said, anticipating what I might say next.

"Well — we had this conversation about friends becoming lovers. Romey believes that best friends can become perfect lovers, but I was not that sure."

"Come on Rachel. What else happened?"

"Mom — will you calm down? And stop interrupting me," Rachel scolded.

Mom pretended that her lips was a zipper and pretended to zip them closed.

"I listened to everything that Romey said because I think that he was trying to suggest that he and I should take that leap of faith. I wasn't convinced then, but later after I got home, I changed my mind. I actually believed that he and I might be able to be together.

Rachel walks over to the couch and plops down. Reliving the events of last night made her feel so stupid and dense, but she regained her perspective and continued.

"After I decided to take a chance with Romey, I went back to the Sequoia and saw him and some woman coming out of the restaurant and he was escorting her to her cab. They were laughing and talking like they were a couple or something. When I saw Romey kiss her on the cheek, I left," Rachel said, burrowing her face in her hands as she sobbed.

Mom came over to the couch and sat down beside me and put her arms around me.

"Oh Rachel — I'm so sorry. But maybe things weren't really as they seemed."

Rachel stopped crying, raised her head abruptly, and shot her Mom an evil glance.

"All I'm saying sweetheart is that maybe things weren't really as they seemed!" her mom explained.

Mom!" I yelled. "I know what I saw! Damn! Are you trying to say that I'm blind too?"

"Of course not okay? — relax now. Calm down Rachel. I'm sorry. I didn't mean it like that. All I'm saying is that sometimes you may not know everything. That could very well not be the whole story Rachel," Mom pleaded.

Rachel stood and walked over to the living room window and stared blankly outside. She leaned her head against the window facing and watched the magnolia tree limbs float with the breeze.

Mom got up and walked over closer to me. She sensed that her mom was disappointed that things didn't work out for her and Romey because she was always a huge fan of his. But it was over now and Rachel felt that she had to except it and her mom needed to do the same.

"Look Rachel, I still say that Romey and you belong together. You know that you love him and he —"

"He what Mom?" Rachel interrupted, turning her head around to face her mom. "He loves me? Was that what you were going to say? Well he showed me just how much last night Mom. He and this woman was together so that's enough for me."

"But Rachel, Romey —"

"I don't want to hear anymore, okay?"

"Rachel, Romey —"

"Mom — I s-a-i-d, I don't want to hear anymore!"

"Okay – fine – fine. I got to go anyway."

Mom turned and headed for the door. "I'll see you tomorrow sweetheart," Mom said, as she closed the door behind her.

A little while later after her Mom had gone home, Rachel went to work on her book and typed until it was very late. She was so tired that she could barely keep her eyes open. She decided to call it quits for the night and work on it again at a later time.

After preparing for bed, Rachel crawled beneath the silky covers of her queen-sized bed. As she lay there, she thought of her book and how great the end product would be. She also thought of Romey even though she had tried very hard not to. He had always believed in her no matter what task or endeavor she pursued. She knew that he would support her decision to write this book about Motown if she told him, but she had decided that she was not going to tell him about it. Her heart says that she truly loves this man, but she also feels that they wouldn't be able to have a future together as a couple. She is in love with him but it is a hopeless cause. Rachel had finally had the realization that Romey would be always in her heart.

Chapter 23

Six months later

Time had flown by and things were very busy for me as I juggled preparations for my media interview in Seattle, Washington and the continued growth of my business. My company was continuing to grow. Tina was promoted and now had her own office and was doing an excellent job as an editor and my assistant.

My book *Forever Motown* ended up being on many best-selling lists including Amazon, Barnes and Noble, and USA Today. All of the media attention had cast me into the literary spotlight and had my fast approaching television interview in Seattle, Washington on a talk show called *Point of View* and I was so excited about it. All of my family and friends were excited to personally know a best-selling author and they all were very proud of me.

Since I had a public relations background, I knew that proper publicity is essential for advancing book sales. Whether preparing for a TV, radio, Internet, print, or face-to-face interview, the basic criteria are the same with only minor variations. I did have to familiarize myself with the format of the news source. I watched, listened to, and read the program where I will be interviewed. I asked questions such as,what type of interview is it? (newsroom, in-studio) how do I need to present myself? How do they sit and handle the microphone? What kind of personal contact is between the interviewee and interviewer? How formal or casual is the interview? I wanted to be prepared. Sondra McDowell was the lady who would do the interview and she had given me some interview questions to help me get organised before the actual interview itself.

Tina, Mom and I went shopping to help me choose a great outfit for my TV debut. We all decided on a very nice blue designer pantsuit with all of the accessories. Somewhere I read that all colors were good for television because they didn't photograph well. I found out that the safest color on television is blue. Contrary to what some people might say, reds also photograph well. Avoid white and avoid black. Always avoid patterns and prints, because they are distracting to people, and the camera can't read them very well. If you're going to have any patterns or prints, for a woman, put them underneath in the blouse, never on the outside.

"You guys, all of this shopping has made me hungry," Tina suggested, rubbing her stomach. "While we're here near these restaurants, why don't we choose one and get a bite to eat," she added.

"That sounds great. I just noticed that it was lunchtime. Where do you want to go?" I asked.

"I really don't have any idea. What do you suggest Mom?" Tina asked.

"Well, what are you in the mood for?" Mom asked. "I think I'm in the mood for pasta. There's a great Italian restaurant not far from here. It's called *Antonia's* and the food is delicious."

"I remember that place Mom. I had almost forgotten about it," Rachel said.

When we arrived at Antonia's, we all went inside. It was a small restaurant, but I immediately knew why Mom likes it so much. The place was elegant and classy, and I was positive the food matched the atmosphere. We all were quickly seated and our drink orders were taken.

We sat at a quiet table near the front window and chatted about the day's events. The waitress returned with our drinks and then took our food orders. After she left, we began discussing my interview.

I was so happy to have my friends here with me helping me and being great friends. I could feel my excitement growing as my interview time approached.

The waitress returned and placed delicious-smelling plates in front of us. I had ordered herb chicken tortellini soup, and at the urging of Mom, joined her and tried the fettuccini with portabella mushrooms, ham, and asparagus. The waitress has set a dish of hot, crusty Italian bread in the center of the table and when she left, we began to eat.

With her first bite Tina exclaimed, "Oh, Mom, this is delicious."

"I thought you would enjoy it. It's my favorite, and whenever I can talk Robert into bringing me here, I usually order the fettuccini," she said as she picked up her glass of red wine and took a sip.

"Rachel how is your soup?" Tina asked.

"It's delicious," I replied as I picked up a small piece of bread.

"I hope that's not all you're eating," Tina said worried.

"It is, but you have to remember that I have an interview coming up and I have to fit into my designer pantsuit. I don't want to gain so many pounds that it won't fit," I said smiling.

"Ah yes, the interview. Here's to you having the most wonderful interview, Rachel," Tina said as she raised her wine glass.

"Yes, the interview we all will be watching," Mom said as she and Tina toasted the media event that would soon take place.

I laughed and continued to eat. At the end of our meal the waitress returned and offered them coffee and dessert. Though I declined, Tina and Mom ordered tiramisu. When the dessert arrived, I couldn't keep my eyes off the tempting dish. As Tina ate, I watched the fork leave and return to her mouth, carrying another bite of the coffee-flavored desert. Finally, I picked up my fork and stole a tiny piece from Tina's plate. Mom and Tina broke out into laughter, as they had both wondered when I would break.

Though their conversation was lively and the meal was wonderful, both had ended too soon, like all good things. Though Mom and I bumped heads on occasion, I still loved my mom very much. She made me furious as hell sometime, but I always knew deep down that she meant well. She still refuses to give in on the idea of Romey and me getting together. The strange thing is that Mom's instincts were right the majority of the time.

After paying their bill and leaving a tip, we left the restaurant and headed home. It had been a long but enjoyable day out with my wonderful friends.

My big day had finally arrived and I was backstage getting prepared for going on camera for my media interview. Sondra came back there and helped me to relax because I was a little nervous. She advised me to just try to remain as calm as possible, to maintain eye contact with her, and to just think of the television set as your living room and to be calm. Sondra also added that I needed to try to relax and to pretend that I was just sitting on my couch at home watching television.

They fastened the small microphone to my jacket lapel and secured a transmitter pack to the back of my trousers and asked me to wait for my cue to come onto the set. I listened as Sondra did her introduction and then I was cued to walk on the set.

The audience cheered loudly as I made my way to where Sondra was sitting waiting for me. I smiled and waved to the crowd as I sat down and Sondra smiled and reached over to shake my hand. So now the interview begins.

"We have on our show today Rachel Pendleton, the President/CEO of Deléna Publishing, but she is also a best-selling author of a book called Forever Motown. This book has been on many best selling lists including USA Today, Amazon, and Barnes and Noble. We are going to talk about Rachel's book, but first I want to give you a little background on this very intelligent woman."

"I have been following Rachel's career for years, and I had no idea I was going to meet her in person until I showed up for the Forbes Executive Women's Forum for a speaking engagement, and there she was, speaking right before I did. She was mesmerizing: funny, authentic, quick on her toes and gorgeous. But I most love her for her honesty. Everyone does; even the Manhattan Times Review board of directors.

This board had played a large role in her getting her job. The short history of Rachel is that she started her career in the Editorial department Manhattan Times Review as a graphic designer, then to editor, and from that to public relations. When the editors started compromising ethics during the dotcom boom she was one of the most high-profile editors who didn't, so her career went into super-high gear during the dotcom fallout. Rachel then relocated to Manhattan where she became Editor and Chief of the Manhattan Times. Now she is President/CEO of Dalána Publishing and is one of the highest-ranking women in that field."

"Okay, Rachel, here is your first question. **"What is a good first job for someone who wants to run his or her own company?"**

"I tell all young people to become an analyst after school. You pull out bits of information and put together a picture. Sometimes it looks like a dog or sometimes a cake. Then you make decisions with imperfect information. And when you get another piece, you say oh it's not a cake. So it's practice on making decisions with imperfect information. This is what you do as a CEO every day. It's a judgment call that you make based on the information that's there."

"Why aren't women at the top of companies?"

"There is something about women getting tired. They get to be thirty and they get tired. Add up all the time that you are not with the kids and not working but you are doing hair and makeup while your husband sleeps. It's two-and-a-half hours a week. It drags you down. Also, women are not able to express anger at work because it reflects negatively on women. This makes women tired, too. Also, some women are afraid to try to advance because of some male chauvinists' opinions that women can't be leaders."

"What's your approach to work/life balance?"

"When women get up there and talk to you about work life balance, I feel that they aren't being totally truthful. I work all the time. I sent 220 emails last weekend. The last time I went out for drinks on a weekday like Sex in the City was when I was twenty-two years old. This is not a bitter comment. It's a choice."

"What magazines/websites do you read regularly?"

"I read them all (even the weekly's I hate to say) – I like to stay in touch with the trends."

"Please comment on how you feel being a woman helps and hinders you as an entrepreneur."

"Regardless of whether they are entrepreneurs or not, most of the women I know juggle more than men. They tend to be great multi-taskers who move mountains for little or no recognition. For instance, most women I know have had to invent solutions to make the work force more accepting of women who want a family and a high powered career. The quest for creative solutions to age-old problems is not unlike that of entrepreneurs who challenge the status quo. Being a woman is great practice for being an entrepreneur!"

"What are the top five qualities you would ascribe to an entrepreneur?"

"I would have to say, self-confidence, being resilience, open-mindedness, being able to follow-through with your goals, and creativity."

"Do you have a mentor who has helped you in your career path/personal development?"

"No, not really, but I do have a best friend, however. This person has been most responsible for helping to encourage my career path and personal development. His name is Roman Sinclair and we have been best friends since we were kids. His unwavering belief that I can do anything "they" can do but better, backwards, and in heels, so to speak, fuels me every day."

"What is the latest insight (about life, work, play) that you picked up and would like to share with the audience?"

"My way, while not the only way, is a good way. One goes through many phases in a life and career and different approaches are required at different times. Knowing when to defer and when to persist is difficult. Making the right choice is a function of experience. At this point in my career, I have enough experience to know which way to go, which is nice."

"We like to ask everyone this question about his or her personal life. Do have a special someone in your life?"

"Unfortunately, I don't have a boyfriend at this time, but I do have a very special male friend who is my best friend. As I told you earlier, we have been best friends since we were kids and there has never been any romantic involvement between us."

"Well Rachel, we have a special guest here today who may challenge what you've just said." Sondra remarked.

Just to my left and few yards away I saw Romey entering the set. I was in such shock and my jaw dropped in awe. The audience was seriously rooting for Romey and cheering loudly as well as Sondra.

In a low tone, I asked, "Romey -- What are you doing here. What are you up to?"

"Relax my love," Romey said with a wink. "I have been waiting for quite some time for this very moment. Rachel to finally be able to admit how I really feel about you is indescribable. Now I have my chance and I want the world to know that I am in love with you and have loved you since back in our college days."

"But Rom —,"

My words were broken up by Romey bending down and planting a gentle kiss on my lips.

Then Romey spun around on his heel and went to meet a gentleman that was making his way on the set with a microphone. Suddenly, smooth, slow R & B music began playing and Romey grabbed up the microphone and walked back over to me. A few moments later, Romey's deep, lush voice with a that silky yet forceful tenor began singing a gentle testimonial of his love and passion for me in a song that was titled *Always in my Heart*.

The song went like this:

> *Every night in my dreams I see you, I feel you*
> *Love can touch us one time and last a lifetime*
> *Nothing can compare to love,*
> *The way it reaches out and grabs you*
> *I just had to let you know that I want to make*
> *you mine.*
>
> *All I want, all I need is you*
> *It doesn't matter what they say*
> *I'm gonna love you anyway*
> *You will be always in my heart.*
>
> *You're such a joy to be around, nothing*
> *compares to you*

*I knew that something magical was going to
begin
The way you look at me let's me tells me I can
trust in you
I can never let you go, because I don't want
this to end.*

*All I want, all I need is you
It doesn't matter what they say
I'm gonna love you anyway
You will be always in my heart.*

*So many guys took your love and let you down
But I'll be the best man for you; I'll always
be around
Take my hand, hold it tight, and never let
it go
These arms will hold you, keep you safe and
warm
And I'll love you always and forever more.*

*All I want, all I need is you
It doesn't matter what they say
I'm gonna love you anyway
You will be always in my heart.*

After Romey finished with his song, he walked over to me and extended his hand to me. I was so moved by this song and by Romey's declaration of love for me that I felt light as a cloud. I had some serious butterflies in your stomach and I felt so much excitement. A hush came over the studio audience as Romey and I shared the sweetest, most sensual and passionate kiss. Moments later the crowd went mad with near hysteria — they applauded, shouted, and whistled — they gave us a standing ovation.

You would think that with so much noise going on around us that it would have had some kind of effect on Romey and me, but it didn't. The two of us were in our own world as we held each other closely and tightly. Now that I know how Romey feels about me, I have a surprise of my own. He's not the only one with something to say. I broke our embrace and took the microphone from his hand. The crowd had calmed down a little and could hear me when I spoke over the microphone and said: "I have an announcement that I would like to make everyone."

Another hush came over the crowd as I prepared to speak.

Now that I know how much this man loves me, I want him to know that I had always been in love with him. I turned to face Romey as I spoke these next words.

"Romey — I have been in love with you since we were back in college but I had tried to convince myself that I didn't love you for all these years. I didn't have the courage back then to admit how I felt about you, but now I do. I know that for the rest of my life that you're the only person that I'll ever want to be with. I have my true love and now I'm never letting you go. So I ask you now — Romey — will you marry me?"

It was so quiet after I asked that question that you could hear a pin drop. But Romey didn't make me wait long for his answer. The crowd seemed as though it was holding its' breath too, waiting for a reply from Romey.

A broad smile adorned Romey's handsome face and then he replied, "Yes Rachel — I will marry you. I'm in love with you girl."

After that night Romey and I were inseparable. About a month later, he and I were married in a quiet, private little ceremony of immediate family and friends. Romey and I couldn't be happier. We share an unconditional love. I love him as he is, as I seek to find my own special way to relate to the world, or the way I feel that is right for me. It is important that I am the person that I want to be and not someone that others think I should be.

Since Romey's solo debut, he has released nothing but platinum records that he not only sang on, but produced, wrote and arranged and recorded with Echo Prism Records. This ultimate singer of songs had a groove that could not be copied – and he didn't copy.

Over the years, Romey refined his craft, broadened his stylistic scope and reached every conceivable audience. His mainstream breakthrough happened with the pop Top 10 success of "Forever in Love," which reached the pop Top 10 and has lived on as a wedding song staple. Romey was emerging as the leading romantic singer of his generation, racking up one platinum album after another and charting several R&B hits, such as ''You are my Fairytale,'' ''Forever in my Heart,'' and ''Love Won't Wait.''

The momentum continued with more Top 10s. " Give Me a Chance," "Can't Be a Fool" and his duet with *Nadia Reed*, " Your Love is Worth the Wait " (a #2 pop smash). Videos to " Is it True Love," " Home is Here with Me " and " What Can Be Better Than Love " remain essential contributions to the libraries of both VH1 and BET, while his songs and productions for many popular song artists measure up against the work of any other pop titan.

On " If Only," his 14th solo album and first for Sadeé Records, **Romey** upped the ante with broader strokes of jazz, funk and dance – sounds that always had been a part of his music – was now Romey-nized and made his own. The balladry that helped all of his previous albums achieve platinum, double or multi-platinum status and generated many of his 22 Top Ten R&B singles is still confidently smooth, and yet intricate and involved. The title track, a gentle testimonial of a passion that defies the status quo, was one of the album's many luxuriant love songs and future pop hits.

Romey even got his first breakthrough in show business when his composition "Everybody Sing Halleluiah " was included in the hit Broadway musical *There's No Church Without Jesus*. Two years later, *David Saxon* asked Romey to arrange and sing backgrounds on his "Young World USA" LP (which also included the Sinclair song " I Can't Say Goodbye") and subsequent tour.

Through Saxon, Romey met *Mimi Barrister*. He sang on her *"Songs For The New World"* album and toured with "Miss B" as a backing vocalist. His reputation grew when he became one of the most popular session and jingle singers.

His career hit an even higher plateau as he released his double-platinum solo debut, "Never Too Late."

Few performers toured as consistently or as successfully as Romey, who did not have to rely on package bills or prerecorded tracks to sell out arenas.

Many best selling musicians seem to experience a moment of great success when their initial style matches the public's taste, then struggle to adapt when the public moves on. Romey was an artist who expressed himself through song and sound, and although he didn't ignore the world around him, he remained true to himself.

Romey had his own perspective on his place in pop/R & B history and think that he will remain there for a very long time.

- What Can Be Better Than Love
- Give Me a Chance
- Forever in Love
- Is it True Love
- Your Love is Worth the Wait
- If Only
- Home is Here with Me
- Deny Love Not
- Can't Be a Fool
- Never Too Late

Roman *"Romey"* Sinclair is fast becoming one of the most successful R&B artists. Not only has he scored a series of multi-million-selling albums containing chart-topping hit singles and perform sold-out tours of the U.S. and around the world, but he also has taken charge of his music creatively, writing or co-writing most of his songs and arranging and producing his records. He also performs these functions for other artists, providing them with hits as well. Romey is currently working on a new album which is titled *"Romey*

– *Reflections of Me."* He is, however, equally well known for his distinctive interpretations of classic pop and R&B songs, reflecting his knowledge and appreciation of the popular music of his youth. Possessed of a smooth, versatile tenor voice, he has charmed millions with his romantic music and me too.

I'm thankful that Romey and I found a permanent place for our hearts at last and I'm so thankful that I found a husband who is so supportive of all. And the one person who stands in a class of his own is my husband Romey. It's no secret to anyone how important his role is in my life. And believe me, I try to remind him every day. I truly consider myself one of the luckiest women on earth.

I wrote a poem that I called *"Nourishment of Love – Food for the Soul.* I have always enjoyed writing and used to be able to write some halfway decent poems. I wrote this poem that I keep in a bible that serves as a reminder of the love that I had almost lost by being afraid. It goes like this:

Do not ever deny love...
Even if it is a forbidden love...

If you allow yourself to feel love...
Especially if it's love by the heart...
This love is the only true food...
That can feed your soul...

For if you starve a soul...
It is the most severe crime...
Against the awareness and deep...
Emotional feelings of all mankind...

So Feast, relish, and take pleasure in...
Feeling and enjoying deep emotional love...
Allow your soul to grow healthy...
Feed freely upon the nourishment of Love...

By
Rachel D. Pendleton-Sinclair

In Dedication...

To my mother, Lula James-Fluker, who has always believed in me.

To my both my sons, DaMarcus A. Parks and DaTerrius L. Keaton, who I love with all my heart and who love me unconditionally.

To my grandparents, John and Estella James, who I always carry in spirit, but showed me how a truly loving marriage can be.

To Kimberly Kaye and 96 KIX FM in Jackson, TN,

Just to share a little information about me, I was born in Marianna, AR. I am a proud graduate of Holly Grove High School, and I am currently working toward a degree in Business Management from Phillips Community College of the University of Arkansas and continuing on to a four-year college to get a degree in Business Administration.

I began my writing career in the High School, when I would hand-write my stories for my classmates to read. I'm proud to say some of those same classmates are Carrie J. Keaton readers today!

My professional writing career began in 2006 when I self-published my debut novel with Authorhouse. **Two Loves, One Heart** is an inspirational novel that explores domestic violence, love, romance, relationships, and friendships. I wanted to reach out to abuse victims to let them know that they are loved and are worthy of being helped. This help can come from family and friends or professionally if the need be. I can speak from experience because I am a **SURVIVOR.**

My strong faith in God and my family helped me to find my way back from that dark and lonely place. I am thankful and truly blessed. That horrible experience has taught me that, **"LOVE SHOULDN'T HURT"**.

I have just completed this wonderfully, inspirational page-turner titled, **Always in my Heart**. Rachael Pendleton and Roman "Romey" Sinclair are two people who connected with each other and have been the best of friends since childhood. But Rachael and Romey share something else — a deep love for each other that neither will acknowledge. Rachael or Roman must find a way to let their inhibitions go or they could lose each other forever.

1. Do you believe that men and women can be just good friends? Do you believe that platonic friendships are doomed because physical attraction always interferes?

2. Rachel has been in love with Roman for years but never told him because of fear of losing their wonderful friendship. Would you have told him how you felt or would you have kept it to yourself? Why?

3. Do you believe that good friends can maintain their friendship even if the sexual relationship breaks down?

4. Rachel and Chris had relationship problems because he believes that women can't be leaders or CEO's of a company and that it's a man's job. Do you think that this way of thinking has momidity? If so why?

5. Many of Chris's chauvinistic comments caused Rachel to doubt herself. Why is that a man can make a woman second-guess herself?

6. Rachel had grown up to be an independent and intelligent woman, but she had allowed her mother to make her resent her older sister Robin because she bragged on her constantly about having a husband and family. Robin abandoned her career to be a mother and wife and Rachel didn't. Was Rachel wrong for holding resentment toward her sister because of what her mother said?

Love is a temporary madness. It erupts like an earthquake and then subsides. And when it subsides you have to make a decision. You have to work out whether your roots have become so entwined together that it is inconceivable that you should ever part. Because this is what love is. Love is not breathlessness, it is not excitement, and it is not the promulgation of promises of eternal passion. That is just being *"in love"* which any of us can convince ourselves we are.

Love itself is what is left over when being in love has burned away, and this is both an art and a fortunate accident. Your mother and I had it, we had roots that grew towards each other underground, and when all the pretty blossoms had fallen from our branches we found that we were one tree and not two.

— **Captain Corelli's Mandolin**

"Love is the beauty of the soul."

— **St. Augustine**

There is only one happiness in life — to love and to be loved.

—George Sand
1804-1876, French Novelist

Women wish to be loved not because they are pretty, or good, or well bred, or graceful, or intelligent, but because they are themselves.

—Henri Frederic Amiel

1821-1881, Swiss Philosopher, Poet, Critic
Pleasure of love lasts but a moment, Pain of love lasts a lifetime.

—Bette Davis

If you love me, let me know. If not, please gently let me go.

—Anonymous

To the world you may be one person, but to one person you may be the world.

—Heather Cortez

The best and most beautiful things in the world cannot be seen or even touched. They must be felt with the heart.

—Helen Keller